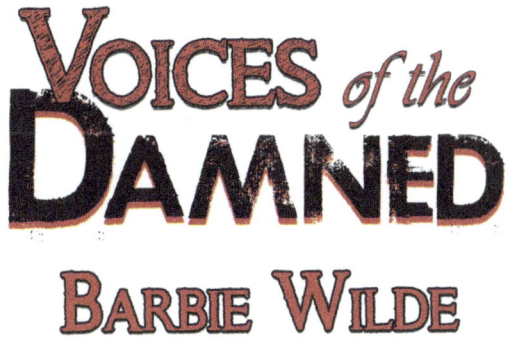

VOICES *of the* DAMNED

BARBIE WILDE

Short, Scary Tales Publications
Birmingham, England

- 2016 -

ISBN: 978-1-909640-36-8

2016 SST Publications Trade Paperback Edition

Published by
Short, Scary Tales Publications
15 North Roundhay
Stechford
Birmingham
B33 9PE
England

www.sstpublications.co.uk

Book design by Paul Fry

Printed in the United States of America and the United Kingdom

First Edition: April 2016

10 9 8 7 6 5 4 3 2 1

ADDITIONAL COPYRIGHT INFORMATION

THANK YOU . . .

Fɪʀsᴛ, I'ᴅ ʟɪᴋᴇ ᴛᴏ ᴛʜᴀɴᴋ ᴛʜᴇ ɪɴsᴘɪʀᴀᴛɪᴏɴᴀʟ Cʟɪᴠᴇ Bᴀʀᴋᴇʀ: ᴀᴜᴛʜᴏʀ, screenwriter, filmmaker, artist, *Hellraiser* creator and one of the reasons that I'm writing horror today.

I also wish to thank some of the most brilliant artistic talents of the horror genre who have generously contributed their luminous artworks to this collection: Clive Barker, Ben Baldwin, Tara Bush, Eric Gross, Steve McGinnis, Nick Percival, Vincent Sammy and Daniele Serra.

Thanks to Paul Kane and Marie O'Regan, who asked me to submit a horror story to the *Hellbound Hearts* anthology way back in 2009. (Even though I told them that I really didn't "do" horror at the time, because I was just interested in writing dark crime. Well, that's certainly changed!) My first horror story was called "Sister Cilice" and it was the beginning of a writing journey that has finally arrived with the publication of this horror story collection. Additional thanks to Paul and Marie for asking me to write a short story for *The Mammoth Book of Body Horror* in 2011, which they also edited.

Thanks to editors Dean M. Drinkel (*Phobophobia, The Demonologia Biblica, The Bestiarum Vocabulum, Phobophobias, The Grimorium Verum*), Kelly Dunn (*Mutation Nation*) and William Meikle (*The Unspoken*) for inviting me to submit stories to their horror anthologies.

Thanks to film directors *extraordinaire* Jen and Sylvia Soska for taking time from their darkly delicious projects to write the Afterword for this collection.

Thanks to Mark Alan Miller, VP of Clive Barker's Seraphim Films.

Thanks to my "ideal readers" Tim Dry and Georg.

Thanks to everyone who has taken the time to read my work and given me such great reviews over the years: Doug "Pinhead" Bradley, *Fangoria's* Chris Alexander, Paul Kane, Jim Mcleod (*Ginger Nuts of Horror*), NY Times best-selling authors John Skipp and Jonathan Maberry, director Jovanka Vuckovic, Gabino Iglesias (HorrorTalk), Blood. E. Bastard (*Horror News Network*), Mandy DeGeit (*Snakebite Horror*), Annie Riordan (*Brutal As Hell*), Jon Towlson (*Starburst* magazine), Larry Darling Jr (*Horror Homework*), Garrett Cook (*Imperial Youth Review*), Johnny Mains, Gabriel Ricard (*Drunk Monkeys*), Michael Wilson (*Scream*: The Horror Magazine), John Gilbert (*Fear* magazine), Paul Simpson (*Sci-fi Bulletin*), Ron McKenzie, Jessa Sobczuk (*Rue Morgue*), Alan Kelly (*Rue Morgue Online*), Lee Allen Howard (*Midwest Book Review*), *The Monster Librarian*, The Church of Satan, Chris Limb (*British Fantasy Society*), James Simpson (*Zombie Hamster*), Chris Hall (*DLS Reviews*), *Bizarre* magazine, *Horror Punks, The Slaughtered Bird, The Horror Honeys, All Things Horror*, Kat Ellinger (*The Gore Splattered Corner*), *The Fright Site, This Is Horror,*

WickerGirl, *Street Sounds*, *Fatally Yours*, *SFX* magazine, *Darkling Tales*, *Promote Horror*, *The Horror Society*, *Fright.com*, Stephanie Hensley (*Traumatic Cinema*), *Horror Drive-In*, Eric Fabiaschi (*Up on the Dark Corner*) and the fabulous reviewers on Amazon and Goodreads. (Apologies if I've missed someone's name off this list.)

Many thanks to Paul Fry of SST for nurturing this project to fruition.

And last, but certainly not least, a special thank you to filmmaker (*Blood for Irina*, *Queen of Blood*, *Female Werewolf*) and *Fangoria* & *Gorezone* Editor-in-Chief Chris Alexander for all the unwavering support he has given my writing over the last few years. It's not easy to make the transition between professions. A lot of people just want to stick you in that "actress" box and not let you out, but Chris has consistently and enthusiastically read and promoted my writing through *Fangoria* and *Gorezone*. And thanks as well, Chris, for writing the Foreword for this collection.

—BW

PRAISE FOR BARBIE WILDE

"Damaged people, ultraviolence, murder and explicit sex—
what's not to love about her work?"—*Fangoria #321*

Voices of the Damned

"Violence, pitch-black humour and yes, sex can be found in equal measure in her work, drawing complimentary comparisons to Clive Barker's early works in his seminal *Books of Blood* collections."—Ron McKenzie, writer at *Thoughts & Scribbles*, *Rue Morgue* and artist (ronniemick at deviantart)

"Wilde has a strong voice. In a genre that is often dominated by male authors, she has taken on a leading role."—Andrew Tadman, *Books of Blood*

"…this collection of eleven short stories confirms Wilde as a foremost author of erotic horror fiction…"—Jon Towlson, *Starburst* magazine and author of *Subversive Horror Cinema: Countercultural Messages of Films from Frankenstein to the Present*

"…her work is so uncanny and fearless, it is a must have for any horror aficionado."
—Writers and directors The Soska Sisters

"Wilde is never one to shy away from verbose analysis of carnal pleasure, and in *Voices of the Damned* she certainly sets the bar high with regards to steamy, gory terror."—
Colin McCracken, *Zombie Hamster*

"Raised from the dead, this phantasmagoria of tales offers well-written mini-nightmares that will traumatize, titillate, and stick in your mind long after you've closed the book."—
Filmmaker Izzy Lee, *Fangoria Online*

"If testosterone jumping erotica combined with heart racing fear is your bag of horror then this is just what you're looking for and *Voices of the Damned* ranks highly in my box of favourites."—Paul Nelson, *Scream Magazine*, *From Dark Places*, *Shelf Inflicted*

Short Stories

"Wilde is one of the finest purveyors of erotically charged horror fiction around."
—*Fangoria*

"Sister Cilice"
(From the *Hellbound Hearts* anthology, edited by Paul Kane & Marie O'Regan, 2009)

"Barbie Wilde's 'Sister Cilice' is devastatingly haunting, piercingly erotic and is one of the true stand-out stories of the anthology."—*All Things Horror*

"Sick, but in delicious ways!"—Doug "Pinhead" Bradley, www.dougbradley.com

"… a potent piece of nunsploitation. It contains plenty of grotesquerie, and, unlike the majority of the book's other tales, doesn't wait until the end to dish it out!"—*Fright.com*

"The Cilicium Trilogy"
("Sister Cilice," "The Cilicium Pandoric," and "The Cilicium Rebellion")

"I've adored Sister Cilice since she made her first appearance in *Hellbound Hearts* and I'm delighted that Barbie's taken her on a journey through two more instalments, completing her arc from sex-hungry nun to one of the major players in Hell; and if you're on the receiving end of her tortures, your suffering will definitely be legendary! She's a Cenobite who gives Pinhead a run for his money, that's for sure. In 'The Cilicium Pandoric' Cilice visits the toymaker for her own puzzle box, the start of her revolution—and in 'The Cilicium Rebellion' she's out to show the men how it's really done, along with her elite band of kick ass female sinners. Intoxicating, bloodthirsty and witty, these are stories to make Clive Barker proud. Anyone who loved *The Scarlet Gospels* will be in Heaven, not Hell, reading these…"—Paul Kane, award-winning and bestselling author/editor of *The Hellraiser Films and Their Legacy*, *Hellbound Hearts* and *Blood RED*

"Z is for Zulu Zombies" AKA "Zulu Zombies"
(*The Bestiarum Vocabulum* edited by Dean M. Drinkel, 2013 & *Gorezone* #29)

"'Zulu Zombies' is pure Barbie Wilde; eccentric, bizarre, dark and frightening but laced with a inimitable, irreverent punk rock exuberance. It was an honor to reprint the tale in the blood-stained pages of *Gorezone* Magazine..."—Chris Alexander, Editor-in-Chief, *Fangoria* & *Gorezone*

"Expect Zulu Zombie mayhem, undead rape, witch doctor rituals, vomiting and plenty of bloodshed. Cram it all into one hell of an adrenaline pumping read—and you've got a strange *I Am Legend* (1954) meets *Zulu* (1964) meets *Horror Express* (1972) maddening ride."—Chris Hall, *DLS Reviews*

"American Mutant: Hands of Dominion" AKA "American Mutant"
(*Mutation Nation* edited by Kelly Dunn, 2011)

"Reading Barbie Wilde has given me pervature of the spine. My eyes weep jizz, and I can't take a wizz without melting someone's face off. Now THAT'S entertainment!"
—John Skipp, *New York Times* bestselling author, editor, zombie godfather, compulsive collaborator, musical pornographer, black-humored optimist and all-around Renaissance mutant.

"A is for Alpdrück" AKA "The Alpdrücke"
(*The Demonologia Biblica* edited by Dean M. Drinkel, 2013)

"Barbie Wilde kicks off the anthology with a weirdly nightmarish short that seems to have been born from the same cast as Clive Barker's 'The Yattering and Jack' crossed with the succubus from James Herbert's novel *Once...* (2001)."—Chris Hall, *DLS Reviews*

"Valeska"

"Especially written for this collection, "Valeska", stands out (alongside the splatterpunk/medical horror "Polyp") as the tale ripest for novel-length treatment (Wilde is currently adapting "Zulu Zombies" into a screenplay – can't wait to see *that* one at the local multiplex), constituting, as it does, a total re-think of vampire mythology."—Jon Towlson, *Starburst* magazine

"U is for Uranophobia" AKA "Gaia"
(*Phobophobia* edited by Dean M. Drinkel, 2011)

"Gaia's story is both powerful and deeply shocking. This tale of latent revenge and pent-up anger was a joy to read."—*Ginger Nuts of Horror*

"A very arty, grim, character study... a slow, steady drift into a heart of darkness climaxing with a buckling level of sex and violence and shock... It's like Von Trier's *Antichrist* and when reading it, I saw Charlotte Gainsbourg as Gaia..."—Chris Alexander, Editor-in-Chief, *Fangoria Magazine*

"Polyp"
(*The Mammoth Book of Body Horror* edited by Paul Kane & Marie O'Regan, 2012)

"Barbie has created a brilliant twist on the creature feature genre. I really enjoyed how the tale went from being a very personal story into an apocalyptic cliff hanger."—*Ginger Nuts of Horror*

"The stories offer icky pleasure for those fascinated with a subgenre concerned with the body turning against itself. Some are funny and disgusting (Richard Matheson's nuclear fallout nightmare ''Tis The Season To Be Jelly!,' Barbie Wilde's bowel-with-a-brain-of-its-own yuk-fest 'Polyp')..."—*SFX Magazine*

"... thanks to Marie O'Regan and Paul Kane for this treasure trove of stories—ranging from some classics in the genre, 'The Tell-Tale Heart,' 'Survivor Type' and 'The Body Politic' to some stories that will almost certainly become classics of their time—the absurdist, very entertaining shocker 'Polyp' to the brilliantly executed 'Sticky Eye'..."—Johnny Mains

"B is for Botophobia" AKA "Botophobia"
(*Phobophobias* edited by Dean M. Drinkel, 2014)

"This is just dark, twisted, sci-fi pulp horror fun. Plain and simple. Now, let's just take a second to ponder what on earth goes on inside Barbie Wilde's mind."—Chris Hall, *DLS Reviews*

"W is for Writer's Block" AKA "Writer's Block"
(*The Grimorium Verum* edited by Dean M. Drinkel, 2014 & *Gorezone* #34, 2015)

"…wildly perverse and stylish…" "A demented gem…"—Chris Alexander, Editor-in-Chief, *Fangoria* & *Gorezone*

"The darker side of the frustrated writer gets a wry, sardonic spin in Barbie Wilde's 'W Is For Writer's Block'… From the film references to the almost comical S & M 'relationship' of the two main characters, to the weaving of the historical with the mythical, to the final twist, it is all presented with dark humour and verve."—Paul M Feeney, *Ginger Nuts of Horror* "The Heart and Soul of Horror"

Reviews of Barbie Wilde's *The Venus Complex*, Comet Press, 2012-14

"After purposefully killing his wife in a car accident, art history professor Michael Friday finds his perspective on things has become a little…warped. Via his personal journal, we're allowed into his mind to slowly watch the disintegration of it, bearing witness to his unnerving sexual cravings and ideas about killing: intertwined with the paintings he loves so much. As Michael writes, he's "turning into something dead"; but at the same time he wants to be somebody, not a nobody.

"Using his diary to rant against the world in general—including everything from banks to popular culture, from national holidays like Christmas to politics—he reveals more about the big, gaping hole in his own life. But as the novel goes on the first person narrative tensely builds up, displaying his dark dreams and innermost thoughts; his way of filling that void and presenting his grisly 'works of art' to the world.

"As intelligent and cultured as *Hannibal*, easily as disturbing as *American Psycho* and infinitely less "reassuring" than *Dexter*, this is a sexually-charged real life horror story that will definitely stay with you."—Award-winning horror and fantasy author, Paul Kane

"I love dark crime, and this is by far the darkest story I've ever read. I felt guilty for enjoying it so much. *The Venus Complex* is tense and fast-paced, dizzying in its bold perversion. But like a serial killer obsessed with his next victim, I could not turn away.

"…Barbie Wilde follows the tradition of Ellis's *American Psycho* and Oates's *Zombie* yet breaks new ground in the field of sadistic crime fiction. If you like the lurid and shocking, you'll love *The Venus Complex*. It's *Dexter*, without a moral code."—Lee Allen Howard, *Midwest Book Review*

"*The Venus Complex* is a delicious collision of noir thriller and visceral horror. Whip-smart devious and jolting!"—Jonathan Maberry, Multiple Bram Stoker Award Winner and *New York Times* best-selling author of *Code Zero* and *V-Wars*

"Wilde expertly charts Michael's diabolical descent into voyeurism, stalking and murder in a transgressive tale that would make Patrick Bateman blush."—Alan Kelly, Hell's Shelves, *Rue Morgue Online*

"*The Venus Complex* is an epistolary portrait of psychopathy as razor sharp as Jim Thompson's *The Killer Inside Me* or Hubert Selby Jr.'s *The Demon*. Disturbing, erotic and powerful."—Jovanka Vuckovic, Author: *Vuckovic's Horror Miscellany, Zombies! An Illustrated History of the Undead* & Filmmaker: *The Captured Bird, The Guest,* Clive Barker's *Jacqueline Ess*

"A novel by a female Cenobite that gives the world a smart, artistic, cynical, cultured serial killer who could give Hannibal Lecter a run for his money. On top of that, this is a poignant, funny, sexually-charged, hardcore critique of popular culture and a deconstruction of relationships, academia, and art."—Gabino Iglesias, *HorrorTalk*, Top Books of 2012

"But I think what I like most about this news story is that she kicked my ass so hard with her first novel. Turns out Barbie Wilde is even scarier than we thought. And that is a terrible, beautiful thing."—*New York Times* bestselling author John Skipp for *Fangoria Online*

"... Hitchcockian in its tale of murderous obsession."—Jon Towlson, *Starburst Magazine*

"Barbie Wilde has crafted a serial killer story every bit as warped as *Level 26*, as exacting as Harris's *Hannibal* series and more sexually adventurous than *Fifty f**king Shades of Grey* could ever hope to be."—Annie Riordan, *Brutal As Hell*

"This is not a novel for the faint of heart and definitely NSFPT (Not Safe For Public Transport), but the skill with which it is written means that some of the darker imagery will haunt the reader long after they turn the final page."—*British Fantasy Society*

"Shocking and explicit, Barbie Wilde's *The Venus Complex* is an intimate tour of Michael Friday's mind as he morphs from a misogynistic, hyper-intelligent university professor into a sexually charged, calculating serial killer. Written in journal form, Friday reveals his most gory necrophilic fantasies, and then makes them a reality. Not for sensitive readers; after finishing this book you might never feel clean again."—Jessa Sobczuk, *Rue Morgue Magazine*

"Wilde is adept in creating true terror by holding up the mirror to our darker side."—*Horror Drive-In*

"This brilliant look into the mind of a serial killer is full of poetic anger and beautiful vitriolic ranting that it makes you wonder from which pit of hell the lovely Barbie came from. In a genre saturated with bland serial killers, and even blander plots, this book shines out like a beacon."—*Ginger Nuts of Horror*, Best Books 2012

Reviews of *The Venus Complex* from Goodreads & Amazon

"A taut, gripping work. Oozing with sinister brilliance."

"Shameless. Sexy. Frightful. Gorgeous."

"… thrilling, erotic and intelligent."

"…sickeningly brilliant."

"The whole thing is so graphically visual, Ms Wilde should have film-makers knocking on her door any day now."

"…thought-provoking and sexy piece of work."

"Gruesomely graphic and sexually explicit, *The Venus Complex* is the very definition of a page-turner."

"…terrific and compulsive reading."

"…twisted and beautiful."

"Visceral And Disturbing…"

For Georg

TABLE OF CONTENTS

FOREWORD

Chris Alexander

I FIRST ENCOUNTERED BARBIE WILDE THE SAME WAY MOST OF YOU reading this foreword did as well: bald, white, pierced and poured into black leather, trailing behind one of the genuine icons of contemporary dark fantasy, seen as a shadow on a silver screen (or cathode-ray illuminated box). Indeed Wilde's presence as Pinhead's right hand, the Female Cenobite in Clive Barker/Tony Randel's *Hellbound: Hellraiser II* was instantly iconic, said performance coming loaded as it did with extra gravitas because of who Wilde was: a lady who was a glowing presence in cinema, music, television and flamboyant pop culture, full stop.

Wilde existed in a dream to me; a fascinating woman and the leader of many lives who I never imagined I would ever meet. But meet I did and, nearly three decades after I first saw her slink around on screen, she's an artist whom I consider a dear friend, someone I admire and care about deeply. When I took over as editor of US horror film magazine *Fangoria*, I had a blast indulging my interests, connecting with performers and creative people that had inspired me as I could now offer them a widely-read platform to tell their stories. Wilde was among the first I pursued. I had learned that she had parlayed her fame as a key member of Barker's cinematic universe into a newly minted role as a writer of psychosexual horror fiction and this added an extra layer of fascination and, if I must be frank, erotic interest. Smart women are my Achilles heel, I must admit and Barbie's cerebral, stylized energy was intoxicating.

So, with that, after some emailed correspondence, Barbie sent me a big box full of books she had contributed to and once received, over the next several days I read many of her short stories. I found her tales to be singular in their dark, sexual, violent, lyrical and atmospheric drive. To know Barbie is to adore her sense of humor, but these tales were grim . . . almost as if her perversions were finding necessary release via her pen, thus causing her to be lighter in "real life." I loved the stories (especially the blistering "U for Uranophobia" [entitled "Gaia" for this collection] which I would love to adapt as a film someday) and, after running a well-received interview in *Fango*, I enlisted Barbie to supply our sister magazine, *Gorezone* with stories.

That collaboration has been a happy one and I'm always thrilled when Lady Wilde releases some new project. Her first novel *The Venus Complex* is about as hardcore a crime fiction novel as you'll read and to see her fans respond so positively to its lyrically vile charms has been a thrill. And now, here in this vibrant collection of wordplay and image, you too can immerse yourself into Barbie's steamy, sanguinary depths, a weird world filled with dreamy imagery, excruciating violence and deviant sexuality, all tempered with a kind of warmth that's hard to pin down. It's almost like, no matter how extreme Barbie's stories get, you can hear her giggling quietly, her bright eyes alive behind her glasses as she paints yet another baroque literary portrait.

Sex, death and madness. Welcome to the world of Barbie Wilde.

SISTER CILICE

(Part I of the Cilicium Trilogy)

"Loved be pain. Sanctified be pain. Glorified be pain!"

FOR MANY YEARS, SISTER VERONICA WAS IN THE SERVICE OF A Higher Power. She prayed nine times a day. Her life was work, prayer, a few fitful hours of sleep, then more work, more prayer. Thousands of her pious words floated up to the ether, but no answer was forthcoming; only a cruel, empty silence.

When her depraved dreams became too overwhelming, mortification of the flesh was the only answer. She remembered the Sainted Father Escrivá's maxim on suffering: "Loved be pain. Sanctified be pain. Glorified be pain!" . . . and so she used the whip with greater vengeance, but although she assaulted her flesh, nothing could chase the demons from her mind, those familiars that had tormented her all her life.

Throughout her childhood, entering an Order was the only option available to her—the one way to cleanse her heart of the many sins her parents were convinced she had committed. "Every sin, no matter how inconsequential, is a blemish on your soul and will lead you to eternal damnation," her mother used to say. According to her parents, her every thought, word and deed was sinful. There was no relief from the guilt. No relief from the remorseless burden of her countless transgressions. And no relief from her rage, which she hid from the world along with her dark fantasies of revenge and pain. Sexual thoughts and acts were forbidden, of course, but that didn't mean these evils left her alone. Perhaps celibacy made it worse, although how was she to know? She'd been sent straight to the Nunnery at the age of seventeen, without even kissing a boy, let alone knowing what it was like to be with a real man in the real world, flesh to flesh. And she would never know.

During her early days in the convent, in an attempt to save her rotten soul, Sister Veronica made the appearance of perfect devotion, to prove to the other Sisters that she had a vocation. Her every act was irreproachable and every word she spoke was blameless. The strain of such unrelenting good behavior, of maintaining such a mask of utter innocence and sanity, was almost unbearable, but her parents—who suffered from an overdose of scrupulosity—had brainwashed her into believing that this was her only way to salvation.

Her predicament got worse when Father Xavier was appointed to celebrate Mass every morning. He was so handsome, so virile, so different from the dried-up, old men that had previously seen to the nuns' spiritual needs. Sister Veronica was convinced that many of the other Sisters felt as she did about him. She could sense their spirits rise when Father Xavier came into the room. Feel the heat from their bodies as they knelt before him as he tenderly ministered the sacraments to them. The occasional accidental touch of Father Xavier's hand on her mouth when he gave her the Host sent little electric shocks through her body. Sister Veronica lived for that random physical contact, even though she knew it was meaningless to him.

Every night, after the others had gone to bed, she would mortify her bare flesh until she bled, but that didn't chase the thoughts of the good

Father away, it just made her suffering more sensual. She imagined that Father Xavier was the one with the lash, beating her senseless. She'd fall to the ground exhausted, bleeding, eyes shut, body completely open and vulnerable, imagining his presence standing over her. Still with eyes clenched shut, she would use the leather handle of the whip, pretending it was him—thrusting inside of her, hurting her. His pain was loved, his pain was sanctified, his pain was glorified. She'd stuff a rag in her mouth to stifle her cries. Sister Veronica came for the first time like that: bloody, naked, sweat-soaked, lying on the cold, stone floor. Momentarily sated, yet forever unsatisfied.

After a while, she refined her technique. To heighten her pleasure, she'd take the end of the whip and wrap it around her neck, pushing the handle deep inside her at the same time; each thrust tightening the lash and ever so slightly cutting off the oxygen to her brain to make her orgasms more intense. She would come again and again, shuddering like an old car dieseling on a frosty winter morning. But the taste in her mouth was bitter, because when she opened her eyes, she was alone. Sister Veronica would always be alone. No man would ever come and fill the dry, empty well of her heart. So she would get up, clean herself, wipe away the tears of anger and frustration, kneel on the cold floor and flog herself again and again for her despicable thoughts and acts.

During the day, Sister Veronica would wear a cilice—a small metal chain with inwardly-pointing spikes—around her thigh. She would pull the cilice as tight as she could without cutting off the circulation. It was supposed to remind her of Christ's suffering, but all it did was bring back memories of her private moments with the phantom Father Xavier. Her sexual fantasies were now beginning to torment her during the day. The irony was she could not make penance and cleanse her soul, because the only person she was allowed to confess to was Father Xavier. So the sins just piled up one on top of the other, multiplying and becoming more putrefied with time.

Then a new scenario began to fester in Sister Veronica's mind. She would confess all her sins to Father Xavier. He would be horrified and drag her out of the Confessional to the altar, rip her robes off and scourge her using a whip with metal tips, degrading her flesh until she begged him to stop. Her cast-off blood would stain the fair linen altar cloth and splatter the faces of the Saints' statues. Then Father Xavier would take her, right there on the marble floor in front of the altar, underneath the enormous suspended golden crucifix. His cassock would fall away from him and reveal the wonders of his flawless body and his sex. She could only imagine what it would look like: ivory in color, hard, and shaped like a Knights Templar sword perhaps. In her fantasies, Father Xavier used not only his saintly member to impale her, but any other implement to hand—the holier the better—to sanctify and cleanse her polluted body and diseased mind. Sister Veronica felt her sanity slipping away, fueled by her feverish, obsessive thoughts. Haunted by her desires, she continued to torment her wretched body until it was laced with scars.

Finally, Sister Veronica asked to be assigned to the library archives in the convent's catacomb-like cellar as a way of calming and cooling off her mind. There were thousands of books down there, ancient papers, letters and epistles, missives from Popes and Cardinals. Perhaps she could immerse herself in history to distract herself from her miserably empty present.

It was there, late one night, that Sister Veronica found an ancient manuscript in an old leaden box whose lock had long since rusted away. It was hidden in an alcove far from the entrance, forgotten for centuries. The box was littered with crunchy long-dead black beetles, a few blood-red, dried roses and a dusty mummified crow; beak open and tongue lolling out as if in accusation.

The book was called the *Grimorium Enochia* and it was written in the 15th Century by Raphael Athanasius. Sister Veronica spent weeks trying to translate the Latin text. For the first time in years, something was taking her mind away from the bloody world of her profane imaginings. She soon realized that she had discovered something far more engrossing than her fantasies. Athanasius was an alchemist, necromancer and cryptographer, and was a friend of the notorious serial killer, dabbler in the black arts, and brother-in-arms to Jeanne d'Arc, Maréchal Gilles de Rais.

At first glance, Athanasius's book appeared to be about his accounts of summoning forth and speaking with angels and demons. However, it soon became obvious to Sister Veronica that his manuscript was far more than just a few incantations and stories. Athanasius's invocations were a pathway into another dimension: a place where the chthonic inhabitants might understand her needs. These beings were called Cenobites and were members of another kind of Order altogether, where pain as pleasure was the norm, not a hidden vice. She was intrigued and hopeful that somehow she might be allowed access into this world, to find an answer to her torment from those who seemed to be fellow travelers.

She knew by now that she was tired of her life, disgusted by it, not because of what she did to herself, not because of her secrets and sins, but because she had always been a slave to other people's demands. She had never been in charge—never allowed to follow her cravings—subject to countless indignities of the spirit. She was soul-sick, but it wasn't her fault. She needed to get out and Athanasius offered her the way. Not back to the real world of pathetic, ordinary people, which she despised because it reminded her of her parents and all those other contemptible, hypocritical sycophants, but moving into a murky, labyrinthine sanctuary of lust, pleasure, pain, power and blood ruled by the un-divine Order of the Gash.

After several abortive attempts, Sister Veronica finally deciphered Athanasius's infernal recipe. Of course, the correct procedure was important, but as she delved into the text, Sister Veronica realized that she already possessed the most essential and vital ingredient for success: the overwhelming desire to invoke the Schism that would allow the Cenobites to enter into this realm and show her their marvels.

She prepared for their entrance with care, finding an abandoned, airless room adjacent to the library where she equipped a makeshift altar with artifacts of torture that she thought would amuse the Cenobites. In the hospital adjacent to the convent, she found a terminally sick child who was too far gone to notice the pint of blood that she furtively collected from him at the fourth hour after midnight. She mixed this with some of her own menstrual blood and poured the mixture into a Chalice that she appropriated from the convent's chapel. She also added her own scourge and cilice as personal decorations to her altar.

As Sister Veronica uttered the final cadence of Athanasius's Latin invocation, she heard the tinkle of chimes, almost too cloying and sweet to her ears, then a mournful bell tolling. The sounds weren't coming from above, but from somewhere near her, down here in the dark catacombs where not long ago, dead bodies of nuns (and as rumor would have it, their illegitimate murdered offspring) were buried. The lights fluttered in time to the bell and she knew that it wasn't just an ordinary power fluctuation. Something, someone, was coming. A twinge of regret stabbed her heart, a touch of panic, but she pushed it away with a mental growl. She was sick to death of fear, tired of being ashamed of nothing, weary of being a weakling. She wanted strength and power and sensation for its own sake. She longed to discipline others, to make them feel as she had. She wanted to be destroyed and remade again.

Another sound entered her mind, the sound of a metronome tick-ing, ticking, ticking—in time to the quickened beating of her heart. The walls of the room groaned in time to the metronome—they bulged and heaved, and between the cracks of the stones, she saw light—a yellowy, sickly, white light. The walls shuddered and she stumbled back to the doorway, ready to make a hasty retreat if her courage failed her. Finally the walls parted, dust erupted in a brownish, rancid cloud—more light spilled into the room, and voices beautiful, but discordant, warbled in the background, like a movie soundtrack played at the wrong speed.

A tall, male Cenobite entered, followed by a few others, but she had no interest in them. She gasped, not in horror, but in admiration. The Leader was stunning, a fallen angel, his princely beauty still shin-ing through, even though his face and body were mutilated and twisted by scars, lacerations, pins, wires and nails. His black eyes were liquid with eternal suffering; eyelids stapled permanently open. His long, black, leather apron was soaked with blood and speckled with bits of flesh. His naked arms were laced with multiple cilices and the razor-sharp, inward spikes poked deeply into his flesh. Barbed wire was wrapped around his chest and chains bound his legs. He held a black leather and steel-capped cat-o'-nine-tails in his gloved hand and she knew who it was for: a special gift just for her. Sister Veronica sank down to her knees and opened her arms wide in a pretty, Madonnaesque pose of gratitude. He smiled, showing perfect bloodied teeth, filed into flawless little points.

A strong, warm wind scented with vanilla billowed up from behind him, knocking Sister Veronica down to the ground. Her robes fluttered up, exposing her secret places and momentarily blinding her. She lifted her arms above her head, and her clothes and veil ripped off and flew off into the darkness, like an enormous, demented crow.

He stared at Sister Veronica—the naked, surrendered nun—and he was still smiling, almost puzzled by her rapt acceptance. He spoke, his voice echoing in the chamber, "Do you know what you are asking of us? Do you know what will happen to you?"

Sister Veronica answered, "Yes, with all my heart. Take me. Make me one of you, if you think I'm worthy. I'll give anything to you. Soul, body, mind, heart. You know they are already yours, if you want them."

He laughed, joined by the others hidden back in the darkness. His merriment didn't frighten Sister Veronica, it just exhilarated her and made her desperate for his embraces. She longed to stand up and go to him, but her limbs refused to move. Sister Veronica felt something tightening at her wrists and ankles, looked and saw silvery, spiked chains pulled tight by unseen hands disappearing into the darkness—stretching her limbs out to their fullest extent, as if she was strapped to an invisible torture rack. The pain of the diamond-sharp spikes digging into her skin was excruciating, but it was nothing compared to the new sensations that were flooding her body. It was as if all her nerve endings were on fire, alert to every mote of dust that landed on her exposed flesh, every grain of dirt being ground into her back and buttocks. She felt like she was being burned at the stake; even breathing hurt—the air stung her lungs. But the pain, instead of being maddening or frightening, just sent her deeper into a bizarre ecstasy. Below her waist, the epithelial fire was flickering up her thighs, then darting inside her—burning her internally with wave after wave of searing, orgasmic thrusts.

Sister Veronica screamed and writhed, pleasure and pain mixed in an infernal cocktail. It was what she always dreamed of, but more. The male Cenobite laughed again, enjoying her delicious agony, and began working his personal magic with his scourge over her naked breasts and genitals. How was it possible to feel more pain? How was it possible to feel more pleasure?

In the shadows, the other Cenobites applauded the show. They hadn't seen anything this entertaining in ages.

The metal hooks on the leather strips of his scourge dug into Sister Veronica's skin and gouged out her flesh. She felt that not only her body was being flayed, but her soul. She didn't care, she desperately wanted release from her old self. She was happy to trade that tired bag of flesh for something else, something beautiful—like HIM. She wanted to be him: intractable, indomitable, powerful, a slave to nothing, but desire. She wanted his nails, pins, wires, fingers and teeth to bite into her, to destroy and then transmute her sad sack of sin into a blood-drenched angel of darkness—the envy of all the other demons. She sent this message to him in her shrieks of horrified delight and gratitude.

He finally stopped and dropped his drenched whip. He walked over and stood astride her body. The pain hadn't abated and Sister Veronica still cried out. He sunk down slowly, a knee planted on each side of her chest and took out a thin-bladed surgical scalpel. He leaned over, placed his hand under her chin and gently pushed back her head. Unable to scream, feet pummeling the ground, Sister Veronica made muffled sounds of anguish as he slowly and artistically carved a new orifice for her. He laced thin platinum wires through her cheeks and, using these as an anchor, hooked and pulled the skin away from her gaping wound. When he had finished, he straightened up and lifted his apron to show her another present he had prepared for her.

The skin fire was nothing. Her bloody wound was nothing. The agonizing whips and chains were nothing. Whatever happened to Sister Veronica next would obliterate her forever, tear her apart and send her whirling down into an abyss of divine degradation, to that special place she had longed to go to for so many years.

The Cenobite entered her, using every orifice, old and new. Sister Veronica's choking, dreadful moans of passion gurgled from her lips, but the sounds were triumphant, and her frantically thrashing body echoed her exquisite feelings of the ultimate in sensual suffering.

Her shadowy Cenobite audience applauded yet again. What a girl! The good Sister's adoration for mutilation, sensation and agony would be legendary, even in Hell.

For many years now, Sister Cilice has been in the service of a Subterranean Power. Hellbound to glory. She has no thoughts, no worries, no guilt, no empathy, no passion, no dreams, nothing to do but to satiate desires that can never really be quenched to the full, but hell, nothing is perfect. She assists her Leader in his work; they are a perfect team. They even finish each other's threats to those who dare call upon them and take turns flaying those unfortunates who thought they knew what they were doing when they summoned the Order of the Gash. Silence from above no longer greets her words, but screams for mercy from below. They pray to Sister Cilice now. They are her supplicants, not the other way around.

The mortification of her flesh no longer gives her quite the pleasure it used to, but the delight in the pain of others is truly enriching. She is no longer concerned about the demons in her mind. She is a demon herself now and woe betide the mind that comes across her.

In a tiny corner of the shriveled, blackened brain that once belonged to someone called Sister Veronica, Sister Cilice hears an echo of one phrase above all others: "Loved be pain. Sanctified be pain. Glorified be pain!"

They are the only words that can still make her laugh.

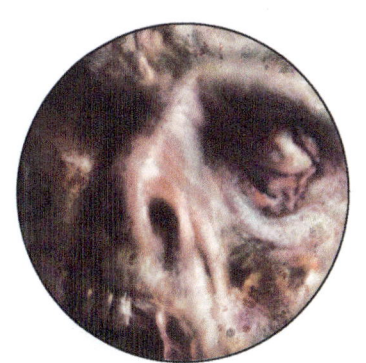

ZULU ZOMBIES

"From Rorke's Drift to Milton Keynes . . ."

IT STARTED OUT LIKE ANY OTHER TYPICAL NIGHT ON THE RAZZLE FOR Trish and Debs, although this time the day and location was Friday evening in Milton Keynes, instead of their traditional Saturday night in Balham. The occasion was a Hen Party for their best mate Sophie and normally they would have stayed in a hotel to sleep off the umpteen Green Apple Martinis they'd consumed, but Trish was meeting her parents for lunch the next day and had to get back to town by the late train to Euston Station at 12:06.

Unfortunately, at the same time when they were supposed to leave for Milton Keynes Central Station, the DJ put on some of their all-time favorite '80s tunes, so they were blissfully dancing next to their handbags to Prince's "When Doves Cry" as their train was pulling out of the station. By the time they arrived on Platform 2, they realized to their horror that the next train wasn't until 03:40. (A minor miracle in itself, considering how most things normally stop dead at midnight in England.)

"Fuckfuckshitfuck!" Trish said, as they shivered barelegged on the platform in their tiny black leather mini-skirts, shiny red stilettos and thin, sequined "Good Luck, Soph!" pink T-shirts. They hunkered together on a bench for warmth and waited miserably on the empty platform.

The drinks soon took effect and in spite of the cold, they fell asleep, only waking when a train was pulling into the station. Bleary-eyed, the two women stumbled towards it, not realizing that Platform 2 serviced both northbound and southbound trains. They were too far gone to notice that they were boarding a northbound train that had left London at 01:34. The train was one of the old-fashioned kind, with doors that had to be opened by human hands, not automatically. After frantically pawing at the handle, they finally managed to fall inside the carriage just as the train started to pull out of the station.

Trish and Debs threw themselves into their seats, giggling madly, pop-eyed and awake because of the adrenalin and fear of almost missing their train.

"Where's the fucking tickets?" Debs slurred and Trish rummaged through her handbag.

"They're here somewhere," Trish said, starting to toss out various rubbishy items like used tissues, tired lipsticks and fuzzy bits of old sweets from the depths of her handbag.

"Must be the fucking milk train," said Debs, staring out the window and noting that their progress seemed achingly slow. She turned around and peeked behind her, spotting some movement down the aisle in the next carriage. "Damn, I can see a Ticket Inspector coming! Find them. Now!"

Trish leaned forward and dumped the entire contents of her handbag on the seat in front of them. Debs laughed hysterically as Trish sorted out her bits and pieces almost robotically. They were both too busy looking for the tickets to notice the Ticket Inspector as he made his way towards them. The lights started to flicker.

Then Trish heard a thud and looked over at Debs. Debs's eyes were bulging and her mouth was wide open. Trish laughed at the ludicrous sight and said, "What's the matter, love. You gonna puke?"

Her eyes dropped down from Debs's face and Trish noticed what looked like the tip of a spear emerging out of Debs's chest. Debs gurgled and spectacularly threw up gouts of blood, then fell forward on the seat in front of them, spraying gore over all of Trish's stuff.

Trish was frozen in fear and shock, too terrified to move, expecting the same kind of treatment any minute. She finally turned around slowly and saw 'it' for the first time. Her jaw dropped and she helplessly peed her knickers in terror.

It was indeed the Ticket Inspector, but his uniform was dirty, blood-stained and ripped. His flesh was the color and consistency of gray, dried-up old oatmeal and his eyes were filmed over with some milky white substance. He smiled at Trish and his teeth were stained black with old blood.

It was that hideous smile that kicked in Trish's survival instincts and she leapt to her feet and fled down the aisle towards the end of the carriage. She came up against the door to the next one and waggled the doorknob, glancing behind to see the Ticket Inspector making his way inexorably towards her.

Trish managed to open the door and make her way to the next empty carriage. She looked around, trying to find something to barricade the door with but no luck. She ran down the aisle and got to the end of that carriage. She was about to go through to the next one when she spotted more weird, white-eyed people slowly moving down the aisle towards her.

Trish was frantic now. She turned around and almost ran straight into the arms of the Ticket Inspector. He grabbed her and dragged her to a seat and threw her down, knocking her head against the metal edge of the top of the seat and stunning her for a moment. Someone grabbed Trish's wrists from behind and lifted her arms back over her head, as the Ticket Inspector knelt down in front of Trish, almost as if in worship.

Trish came to as he ripped open her T-shirt with both hands, exposing her breasts. He briefly touched them, then let his hands trace down her body until he got to the hem of her skirt. He pushed the skirt up, ripped off her soaked knickers and forced her legs open. "No, No, No!" she moaned, as he leant forward and thrust his face in between her thighs. She felt his cold tongue inside her and nearly vomited. She struggled against the person who was holding her arms and looked up to see who it was. Recognition made her turn and throw up violently on the seat next to her.

Debs, still with the spear coming through the front of her chest, was the one holding Trish's wrists. Her face had turned a pasty shade of gray and her eyes were also covered with the milky white substance. Trish spat out the last of the sick and looked up at her former friend. Debs smiled at her as a long stream of bloody drool streaked down from her mouth and splashed Trish's forehead.

Trish began screaming in earnest now, kicking her legs out at the Ticket Inspector. She glanced down the aisle and realized that her situation was hopeless. There was a line of the things now: dead-eyed, oatmeal-faced, blood-stained and dirty—formerly human passengers and staff—standing there patiently, staring at her, waiting to have their turn.

Trish stopped struggling . . . it was more than her mind could cope with. She didn't want to think in clichés, but maybe this was just some kind of crazy, Apple Martini-induced dream. Maybe she and Debs were still asleep on the bench in Milton Keynes.

Then the line of zombies, because that's what they were—no denying it now—lifted up their right legs as one and stomped the ground:

"whomp!" Then they began to sing in a language that Trish didn't understand. Again as one, the line bent down to pick up long cowhide shields that must have been hidden on the floor in front of the seats. With eerily perfect choreographed movements that Bruno Tonioli of *Strictly Come Dancing* fame would have admired, the zombies began to beat their shields rhythmically ("chuka, chuka, chuka!"), at the same time as stomping their feet: "Whomp! Chuka, chuka, chuka! Whomp! Chuka, chuka, chuka! Whomp!"

Trish felt on the verge of having a heart attack with the fear and insanity of it all. The Ticket Inspector stood up and unzipped his fly and his stiff dead purple penis thrust itself out of his trousers. Debs pulled Trish up by her arms some more, bending her backwards over the top of the seat, so the Ticket Inspector could kneel on it. He lifted Trish up by her thighs and entered her, as the others sang and stomped and rattled their shields in deathly excitement.

The Ticket Inspector starting pumping and Trish screamed again as he spilled his churning acidic seed inside her, causing her to have one of the most profound and yet horrific orgasms of her life. The shocking ecstatic internal pain caused her mind to spiral into unconsciousness, but not before a bizarre memory popped into her brain: watching the movie *Zulu* with her dad years ago on a rainy Sunday afternoon. The songs and sounds that the zombies were making echoed those of the Zulus in the film, just before the warriors attacked the 150 British soldiers bravely manning the station at Rorke's Drift in the British Colony of Natal, South Africa, in 1879. Michael Caine's face, complete with white colonial pith helmet, floated into view. Just as Trish was blacking out, she heard him say: "it sounds like a train . . ."

48 hours before the events on the "Zombie Train" . . .

John Jones wasn't looking forward to moving. He was used to the local haunts and pubs that he frequented around his charming flat near Euston Station, but he just couldn't sustain living in London any longer. He felt bad, as the flat had been in the family for nearly a hundred and thirty years, but what could he do? He'd lost his advertising job, the recession was hitting hard and the divorce had pretty much eaten up his savings.

Although he didn't have a buyer yet, the best way for John to make the time pass was to sort through his possessions. The great cull had already happened after the divorce, of course, but there was still tons of his family stuff that he had to get rid of. Hey, maybe some of it was worth something. Interesting artefacts were put in a box for a trip to Sotheby's or Christie's for evaluation. After all, his family had a pretty impressive background—there were boxes full of medals for heroism—although the gene for sterling military service had petered out long before it got to him.

Going through yet another mildew-ridden box one day, John came across the crudely made and mysterious "spirit bottle" of Jones family legend. He remembered when he was a kid gazing at up it on the mantelpiece when his grandfather occupied the flat, before the old boy died, and his mom and dad moved in.

It was really more of a stone jug with a sealed metal plug in the top than a bottle. When he was tall enough, he often sneaked into the living room and gingerly handled the bottle, shaking it to hear a strange hollow rattling sound from within and trying to pry open the plug. Once, his grandfather caught him and John could barely comprehend the rage on the old man's face as he grabbed the bottle and put it on top of a bookcase, out of the curious child's reach.

"Never, never, never touch the spirit bottle!" Grandfather shouted. "Never open it! It is forbidden, understand? All it contains is pure unadulterated evil!"

The little boy ran out of the room, determined to never speak to the crazy old bastard again. Years later, after Grandfather's death, John tried to get the story of the spirit bottle out of his father (what kind of spirits had it contained: whiskey, gin or vodka?), but his dad just shrugged, saying it was just an old wives' tale, not giving out any details.

So there it was . . . in his hands again finally after all these years. It certainly looked venerable enough—sepia-colored, greasy and covered in strange blotches. John dug through the box, hoping to find something that might explain the provenance of the spirit bottle. Two more boxes later, he came across an old letter dated 1880, which caused him a frisson of joy—more money from a possible auction perhaps? Then he started to read the letter and had to pause at one section, because the contents seemed utterly preposterous.

It was common knowledge in the family that one of their ancestors, Robert Jones, had bravely acquitted himself beyond the call of duty at the battle of Rorke's Drift in 1879, actions of which were popularized in the 1964 film, *Zulu*. However, there had been rumors over the years that Robert's subsequent life had not been so exemplary. It was almost as if there was a black cloud hanging over him ever since the battle. Robert settled down in South Africa and married, but his wife died a year later and he soon became bankrupt, losing his farm in the bargain. It was almost as if he was cursed in some way.

The letter, from Robert to a friend called Charles Wainwright in London, was still in its envelope, stamped but never posted. In it, Robert told Charles that he had discovered the reason for his run of bad luck and how he had managed to solve the problem. Robert visited a sangoma, a local female witch doctor, who after a "casting of the bones" ceremony, informed him that the zombie spirits of the hundreds of Zulu warriors he and his comrades had killed during the battle had attached themselves to him and were causing all his sorrows.

To John's bewilderment, he read that Robert put himself completely in the hands of the beautiful sangoma. He endured the cleansing ritual, which included drinking caustic emetics, eating herbal potions and even sacrificing a goat and drinking its blood to satisfy the angry spirits. However, nothing worked, so the sangoma bravely put herself through a grueling purification ritual. She managed to conjure up the Zulu Zombie spirits and then imprisoned them in the stone bottle for all time. She told Robert that he must never open or try to destroy the spirit bottle, because the zombies would issue forth, possess living humans and cause the most horrific mayhem.

Robert gratefully gave the sangoma what was left of his money, which could have proved disastrous, but his fortunes soon turned around and he left South Africa with a substantial sum a few years later, taking the bottle of unquiet souls with him. He later used his riches to buy the family flat just south of Euston Station.

John was thrilled to discover the letter. He was positive that the colorful contents would snare a buyer at auction. After all, a hero of one of the most famous battles in British history going to a comely South African witch doctor to solve his problems? Brilliant. John resolved to take the letter into either Christie's or Sotheby's tomorrow. Who knows? Maybe he could earn enough from auctioning off the letter so he wouldn't have to sell the flat?

Later that night, John was in bed asleep. He was dreaming that he was in bed asleep (always a disconcerting sensation) and that the unquiet

Zulu spirits inside the stone bottle were calling to him, singing strange songs and beating their shields. John was suddenly possessed of the most debilitating terror and he woke up from the dream in a cold sweat. But the sounds didn't stop; they just got louder and more insistent.

John got out of bed to investigate. Maybe it was crowd of rowdy "disaffecteds" in the street that he was hearing, but the noises seemed to be coming from the living room, where John had temporarily restored the stone spirit bottle to its traditional place on the mantelpiece.

He turned on the lights to discover that the bottle was moving, trembling slightly, as if something within was struggling to get out. He ran over to the fireplace and caught the bottle just as it was about to topple off the mantelpiece. He was shocked to feel thrumming vibrations emanating from the bottle.

John was frantic. The last thing he wanted was a bunch of angry undead Zulu zombie spirits bursting out of the bottle and attacking him in his home. He rushed over to the window and threw it open with one hand. The bottle was vibrating so violently now that he could barely keep his grip on it. More in despair than using any rational thought, John launched the bottle with all of his strength out of the window, hoping that he could throw it across the street over the fence and onto the well-kept lawns of St. Eustace Square, but unfortunately throwing was not his strong suit.

The bottle crashed onto the pavement opposite his flat, releasing a cloud of white dust just in front of a young couple walking back from the pub. The man was incensed. He looked up, shook his fist and yelled, "Fuck you, you bastard!"—but his attention was soon distracted by the screams of his companion, who had fallen to the ground and was violently thrashing around. The man bent down to help her, but the woman rose up as if some invisible force was pushing her from behind and attacked him, tearing out his throat with one swipe of her hand. The man dropped to the ground, spouting blood from the wound in his neck.

The woman stopped dead and then looked up at John. She smiled. Even from across the street, John could spot that her eyes were glistening white, no pupils. He jumped back, shut and bolted the window and closed the curtains. He slipped down the wall and cowered in a fetal position on the floor, dreading the thought of a zombie woman pounding down his door and ripping his throat out, but she never came for him. He eventually fell into an uneasy sleep.

Late morning sunshine was striking across the parquet floors when John awoke. What a crazy dream he'd had! Then he glanced up at the mantelpiece and noticed that the spirit bottle was gone. His heart sank as he realized that 134 years of stewardship of the bottle had been broken by one moment of dream-induced panic last night.

John went over to the window, opened the curtains and saw police vans and an ambulance parked across the street. It was real. It really hadn't been a dream. Oh fuck.

Then he noticed that there weren't any people around the vans or the ambulance. The usual assortment of rubberneckers who magically appear at every accident also weren't in attendance. What was going on?

John leaned forward and noted that there didn't seem to be anyone on the streets. They were deserted. Not even a dog taking a shit in the park could be seen.

John sat down on the floor again and tried to think. Whatever was going on was beyond his meager powers of deduction, that's for sure. He spent the day racking his brains for a solution. It was only as evening drew in that John remembered the woman upstairs. He'd only passed her a couple of times in the entrance hall, but his ex had mentioned her a few times. The "Spooky Maven," she called her, a real boffin type, a witchy Internet geek and all around know-it-all.

He went into his bedroom, grabbed Robert's letter and stuffed it inside his shirt. John slipped out of his flat, locked his door and then climbed up the stairs two at a time to the top floor. He got to the landing huffing and puffing and then looked down the stairwell. Again, all was quiet. Then he pounded on the Spooky Maven's door.

"Who the fuck is that?" said the not-so-encouraging reply to his repeated hammerings.

"Hello, ummm . . ." John stammered. Unfortunately, he had no idea what her name was, but then he spotted a small white business card thumb-tacked to the door that simply said "Adendorff" and called out: "Please, Mrs. Adendorff. Open the door. It's Mr. Jones from 3D. It's an emergency."

John heard grumbling behind the door and it was eventually flung open by a short, angry, middle-aged woman with frizzy blonde hair and enormous blue eyes. "It's Miss, if you don't mind. And what the hell do you want?" she asked.

John opened his mouth to reply, but the only sound they both heard simultaneously was a sudden and terrifying "whomp!" coming up from the stairwell, followed by an equally mysterious "chukka, chukka, chukka!" John didn't know what was causing the noises, but it sounded severely ominous. He pushed his way past Miss Adendorff, dragged her inside and slammed the door shut. He locked and bolted the door and turned around to see that Miss Adendorff had armed herself with an ancient, but well-oiled Martini-Henry breech-loading rifle. (John only recognized it because he'd watched the film *Zulu* the other night in a fit of nostalgia.)

"Wait a minute," said John, afraid that he was going to get his head blown off before he could begin to explain his predicament.

"You have two minutes," said the determined woman, her rifle never wavering from the center of John's face.

John rapidly explained the events of the previous 24 hours: Robert's letter, the Zulu Zombies contained in the family spirit bottle, throwing it out the window, the horrors down on the sidewalk. He thought that Miss Adendorff must think he was a lunatic, but as his story frantically spilled out of him to the accompaniment of the approaching "whomps" and "chukkas" from downstairs, the rifle's muzzle slowly lowered.

Miss Adendorff put the gun down on a sideboard, turned to John and said, "Now I recognize you, Mr. Jones. And I'm probably the only person in London who would believe your story."

John nearly collapsed with relief, although what exactly this strange little woman could do to help him out this mess was debatable.

Then something slammed against the door and the "whomps" and "chukkas" were almost deafening. John screamed like a little girl, but Miss Adendorff walked determinedly to the door and looked out the peephole. At first, she couldn't see anything, then a horrible dead-white eyeball filled the peephole. She shut the peephole cover and jumped back as something slammed up against the door again.

"Come on," she told John and strode purposefully into the living room. She shut the door after John to cut down on the racket coming from the landing and walked over to her computer desk.

"Aren't you afraid that they're going to get in?" John asked.

"Even Zulu Zombies would have a hard time forcing their way through the reinforced steel on the door and the frame. I've also had Murray locks installed, so good luck to the bastards, that's all I can say," Miss Adendorff replied.

"So what are we going to do?" John asked.

"You're not the only person who is linked to the events of January 28th and 29th, 1879. My ancestor, Gert Adendorff, was the Boer advisor to Lt. Chard and Lt. Bromhead during the siege at Rorke's Drift. After the battle, Gert suffered from the same problems as your predecessor. Gert was also assisted by a sangoma and our family possesses a spirit bottle as well, although we have taken much better care of ours, it has to be said."

"But that's crazy," said John. "What's the chance of two people with ancestors from that one particular battle living in the same building in London?"

Miss Adendorff smiled grimly, "What makes you think it was chance? My family has taken it upon ourselves to guard the heroes who saved the day so many years ago. I've always known about your history, my friend.

"The Zulu Zombies will eventually go away at dawn. We have to find where they rest during the day—someplace abandoned. Estate agents call them 'zombie houses.' Little do they know how accurate that phrase is."

"Why do they have to rest during the day? After all, they're not vampires." John said.

Miss Adendorff replied, "Because they're tired. They get energy from the moon and the blood they consume and, of course, from zombie sex."

"Sex!?"

"These particular zombies are hungry for it. It's how they regenerate. They will find a suitable live woman and impregnate her, mark my words. Then we will have hell to pay."

At this point, John's brain went "tilt" and he had to sit down in one of Miss Adendorff's overstuffed armchairs, while she went over to her computer and began to rapidly Google deserted properties in the area, eventually coming upon a former monastery behind Euston Station that had been on the market for years. She stared long and hard at the photographs. So long that John went over to her and saw that she was almost in some kind of trance.

Miss Adendorff stood up decisively, pointed at the screen and exclaimed, "This is the place!"

"How do you know?" John said.

"I channeled my ancestor Adendorff, that's how."

"Channeling? Are you kidding? The Zombie House could be anywhere in the city."

"The Zulu Zombies will always be attracted to safe houses near railway stations. This goes back the time of the formation in 1872 of the South African Cape Government Railways, which built the train lines to transport workers across the country. Some evil witches took over some of the trains, turning ordinary workers boarding the carriages into zombies."

Miss Adendorff bustled into another room, dragging John with her. The room was painted dark red and one wall was covered floor to ceiling by an old oak bureau festooned with hundreds of small drawers, all with brass nameplates containing cards labeled in spidery handwriting. She rapidly chose her weapons of war for the coming battle: 9 pieces of broken mirror, 9 straight pins, 9 regular nails and 9 small razor-sharp spearheads.

Miss Adendorff also selected a large-necked stone bottle with matching metal cork, a black candle and some powders of undetermined origin. She placed all the items on a large oak table in the middle of the room, along with a small charcoal brazier on top. She left to go to the kitchen and soon returned with a milk bottle full of a noxious looking red gloop.

Miss Adendorff picked up a small plastic cup and handed it to John.

"Now, I want you to piss in this, there's a good chap."

"You must be joking! I'm too scared to pee."

"Oh, do hurry up. The ritual must be performed at dawn tomorrow."

"How much do you want?" John asked.

"Just fill the cup, will you?"

John peed with difficulty in the privacy of Miss Adendorff's bathroom. She then carefully ladled 9 tablespoons of John's urine into the stone bottle. She gingerly dropped the bits of mirror, pins, nails and spearheads into it as well, all the while mumbling under her breath in a language that John couldn't identify.

Miss Adendorff handed John the milk bottle full of red gloop.

"I want you to drink this all in one gulp. It will make you feel sick. Feel free to vomit."

"What is it?" said John, grabbing the bottle.

"Goat's blood, the purifying drink of choice for all good sangomas, as well as the victims of any curse."

"That's disgusting!" John said.

"So is having your throat ripped out by a zombie. Drink it. It's an emetic, so it will make you throw up almost immediately."

John felt his gorge rising, but there was nothing for it but to follow the Miss Adendorff's instructions. He drank the foul, coppery-smelling stuff, tried to manfully hold it down for the grand total of 2 seconds, then puked up the lot into the large metal bowl that Miss Adendorff had thoughtfully provided.

While John gagged and retched, Miss Adendorff carefully spooned out 9 tablespoons of vomit mixed with goat's blood into the stone bottle. She lit the brazier and threw some of her magic powders on the charcoal, causing a gruesome odor, all the while reciting what John supposed must be invocations in the Zulu language. She waved the bottle over the smoke, softly spoke some enchantments into it and then put in the stopper.

"What's that going to do?" John asked, "Scare them away?"

"No. The Zulu Zombies will be helplessly attracted to the mirrors, the pins, the nails, and the goat's blood. And then, the *pièce de résistance*: the urine and vomit of their enemies."

Miss Adendorff packed a small leather doctor's bag with an ancient revolver, the spirit bottle, a flashlight, the black candle and candlestick, some matches, a white paper bag full of some powder, a machete and a few tools. She adorned herself with some colorful Zulu necklaces and bracelets.

As soon as the sun's rays began to peek over the buildings on the east side of St. Eustace Square, the banging on Miss Adendorff's door, the "whomps" and the "chukkas" died away. John went to the window and saw a stream of people heading north, looking all the while like ordinary Londoner commuters.

Miss Adendorff and John made their way out of the building and through the empty streets. Within five minutes, they were facing a venerable old Franciscan monastery that had seen better days. They walked down a passageway and came upon a side door that was hanging open. Miss Adendorff took out the pistol from her doctor's bag and gave it to John, after taking off the safety catch. She pulled out the spirit bottle and uncapped it, placing the stopper safely in her pocket and transferring it to her left hand. Then she took out the flashlight. She looked into John's face.

"Are you ready, my friend?" she said.

John looked into her surprisingly beautiful eyes and thought that he never felt so unready in his life, but what the hell.

"Let's go!" John replied.

"That's the spirit!"

They entered the monastery. The door was actually an entrance way into the old chapel, which had been decommissioned long ago—no religious symbols could be seen anywhere.

John then became aware of a melodic drone-like sound, a chilling "whoooo-whoooo, whoooo-whoooo" that brought up the hairs on the back of his neck.

Miss Adendorff reassured him, "That's their sleeping song. Not to worry."

Right, thought John. I'm entering a monastery full of Zulu Zombies in the middle of London, but I shouldn't worry.

Miss Adendorff calculated where the exact center of the chapel interior was and knelt down. She took all her weapons out of the leather bag, in preparation for the ritual.

"Keep watch, John," she said. "If any of them come at you, shoot them in the eyes; that will slow them down."

Miss Adendorff began to slowly rock back and forth, joining in the zombies' "whoooo-whoooo" drone.

Then she suddenly called out a summons to her ancestor Adendorff, as well as to the zombie spirits:

AmaDlozi Adendorff, come to me now!
Help me banish those who you vanquished so long ago.
Zulu Zombies—be no more
See these things and end your war

Mirrors that reflect—reflect your souls
Pins that prick—prick your souls
Nails that stab—stab your souls
Spears that pierce—pierce your souls
Mirrors and pins and nails and spears

Reflect and prick and stab and pierce your souls
So you cannot escape your fate . . .

In reply, the Zulu Zombies' "whoooo-whoooo"s cut off suddenly and turned into wild and angry chants. John was startled to see ghostly figures slide towards them out of the darkness and they were soon surrounded by growling, drooling zombie Londoners, who stomped their feet, sang Zulu war chants and hammered cowhide shields. (And where the hell had they gotten those, he wondered?) For some reason, the zombies held their position and did not attack.

Miss Adendorff rose to her feet, holding the white paper bag. She grabbed a handful of the white powder, which John now recognized as salt and threw it in a vast circle, striking as many Zulu Zombies as she could in her first throw.

Raising her voice to be heard over the war chants, the "whomps" and the "chukka, chukka, chukkas," she screamed:

Consume the salt that purifies . . . purifies your souls
Salt that freezes—freezes your souls
Salt that traps—traps your souls
I banish you to the place of dreams
To this umuzi, I send your screams
Zombie spirits of '79
Bother us not another time!

At the last line, Miss Adendorff threw the bag up so the contents flew above all their heads. The Zulu Zombies screamed as one and metamorphosed into white powder.

Miss Adendorff yelled, "Hold your breath, don't breath them in!" then dropped to her knees and grabbed the bottle, crying out another spell in Zulu. The zombie spirit powder, for a moment suspended in the air, was sucked into the bottle as if it was an ectoplasmic vacuum cleaner. Miss Adendorff promptly plugged the bottle with the metal stopper.

"Bloody hell, that was fucking fantastic," John said. Miss Adendorff turned to him and smiled triumphantly, but it was short-lived, as a spear suddenly thrust through her belly from behind. She looked down in surprise and then dropped to the ground, revealing the last remaining zombie who had somehow escaped her spell. John, furious, fired the gun repeatedly into its eyes, which exploded in a most satisfactory manner. Then he grabbed the machete and chopped the creature's head off in one blow.

John glanced around but he couldn't spot any more zombies. He ran over to Miss Adendorff, who was still alive. He cradled her in his arms.

She opened her big blue eyes, smiled, and said, "We got them, didn't we, John?"

"Yes, Miss Adendorff, we did. You were magnificent."

"Call me Della, please."

"Of course, Della."

"One more thing, John. Never in my life . . ." (Della paused for a minute, time was running out for her, John could tell.) "Never in my life have I been kissed by a man. Would you kiss me, John, before I go and join my ancestors?"

Tears popped into John's eyes. "Of course, Della. It would an honor to kiss the bravest woman I've ever met."

John gently kissed Della's lips. A little sigh escaped from her mouth and when he looked up into those extraordinary blue eyes, he could tell she was gone.

He gently lowered her body to the ground and gathered up her accoutrements, taking special care with the spirit bottle. He took the candle and dripped black wax around the stopper, so it was sealed tight.

Never again would these angry spirits of death and destruction escape their prison.

John looked around carefully. Except for the decapitated zombie and dear Miss Adendorff, the chapel was empty. He resolved that the best thing to do was to leave them there and call the police anonymously from a phone box. There was no way he could explain what had just happened, without incurring unfortunate repercussions. He just thanked his lucky stars that Miss Adendorff had captured all the Zulu Zombies in the spirit bottle for good, before anything really horrible had happened.

Not all the Zulu Zombies, of course. As we know, some of them managed to catch the train. The 01:34 to Milton Keynes, in fact. Arriving Platform 2 . . .

AMERICAN MUTANT

"The Hands of Dominion"

As humans dance their merry, destructive way through time, they pretend to know the difference between Good and Evil. They think of Good and Evil as intoxicating outpourings from deities that are as crazed as they are. God, or the Devil, or whatever they believe in, lives on in their minds. But I am the physical manifestation of both. Good and Evil live within me and are separate from any ruling divinity.

I have now been reborn in the light from the darkness. I will carry on the work of my father and it will be good.

—The Gospel According to Mikey (aged 13 and a half)

THE REVEREND BILLY BOB BANNON WAS SMOOTH ALL OVER: smooth-talking, smooth looking, even his outfits were . . . well . . . smooth. He dressed smart casual in gleaming white: white jeans, white long-sleeved shirt, white tie (decorated with discreet little silver teardrops symbolizing the suffering of Our Lord), white linen jacket, white leather belt with a silver buckle, white patent leather loafers with little silver chains and white socks—all of which matched his pearly (and not so natural) white teeth and glowing bleached blond hair. All this gleaming whiteness set off his tan perfectly. And no orange, sun-bedded, George Hamilton skin tones for Billy Bob. No, his tan was real honest-to-goodness (no pun intended) exposure to the sun.

Billy Bob was a dauntingly charismatic individual. He rose from revival tent poverty to owning his own cable TV company in just over five years—admittedly, not a major one, but "big oaks from little acorns grow," as Billy Bob was fond of saying in his fake southern accent. His views—religious, political or otherwise—were ridiculous and overblown, but his flock adored him as much as liberals avoided him. His weekly Sunday morning TV show, *Billy Bob on the Box!*, was a modest hit in Southern and Mid-Western states, and the gullible would send him their crumpled, grimy dollar bills in smudged envelopes whenever he demanded it of them, which was on a day-to-day basis. (And don't forget Billy Bob's daily radio show, *On the Air with Billy Bob!*)

Billy Bob was a success, but it was lonely at the top. His wife Susanne left him for a vacuum cleaner salesman during the lean years and it was tough to find a woman who wasn't either: a) a religious maniac, b) a rabid fan, or c) a prostitute. Not that he had an aversion to fallen women, on the contrary, he had a great appreciation for working gals, but he had to keep his distance. After all, he didn't want to go the way of the Swaggarts and the Bakkers—having it all and then blowing it to Kingdom Come just because he couldn't keep his pecker in his pants.

Of course, deep down, in his shriveled, blasted, hockey puck of a soul, Billy Bob was about as religious as a mongoose. It was all showmanship to him and if his parents had any real money, he would have gone to Juilliard, studied to be an actor and gone on Broadway. But thanks to Jesus & Co., he still got to act a little.

All was going swimmingly if it hadn't been for that one fateful night when he was in Biloxi doing a diabetes telethon. The telethon had gone like gangbusters and he'd pocketed his usual fat fee. After a rewarding stint at the hotel bar with a few ice-cold vodka martinis, he nestled into the nice, cool, cotton-rich sheets of the Holiday Inn's best king-sized bed.

Billy Bob closed his eyes and conjured up the last call girl he'd been with. Years ago it was—after Susanne and before the crazy success had kicked in. Her name was Tiffany and she was a hot little redhead that some hotel concierge in Kansas City had summoned after a desperate 2 a.m. plea from Billy Bob. Tiffany was a nightly guest in Billy Bob's mind ever since and over the years, her boobs had grown bigger and her juicy smile wider. Man, she was sweet and Billy Bob imagined her diving under those cotton-rich sheets and enthusiastically gobbling up his Johnson. A little groan escaped Billy Bob's lips and he grabbed said Johnson, fully intent on rubbing his chubby into acquiescence and himself into a sound sleep.

Then he heard a little noise, like a dry cough. One eye squinted open and all activity under his sheets ceased. A woman was standing at the foot of his bed.

Holy Roller levitation was not Billy Bob's speciality, but it almost looked like it as he leapt out of the bed.

"Who the fuck are you and what are you doing in my room," he sputtered, before noticing the boy standing next to the woman.

"Language, Billy Bob, language. There is a child present," the woman gently scolded.

Billy Bob, his mind befuddled by the martinis, tried to take in the scene. There was something familiar about the woman. She was as redheaded as his dream girl Tiffany, but she looked plum worn out. Attractive, but frumpy at the edges, not like the hard-bodied little number of years past. He looked at the boy, who was ginger-haired, blue-eyed and freckled, obviously her son. The kid smiled at him and he felt a chill.

He knew that smile, having seen it too many times in the mirror. Oh yes, a smile of infinite charm and absolutely zero sincerity. Billy Bob felt trouble brewing: child support payments, scandal, his wonderful, cushy life draining down the plughole. Damn it to hell.

"What do you want?" Billy Bob demanded.

"What do you think I want?" Tiffany replied. "I saw the look in your eyes. You know who I am and you know the boy is yours. Easy enough to prove nowadays with all that DNA stuff."

"Thought you were on the pill, girl. You were a professional."

"Oh yeah? And you should have worn a condom, like I asked you," she shot back.

"Why now? It must have been over twelve years ago, Tiffany."

"Thirteen, actually. Well, I stuck it out as long as I could—all that parenting shit—but I've had enough of this kid. He's yours now. I don't want anything to do with the demonic little fucker. Maybe you can exorcise him in the bargain."

"Whoa, mamma," Billy Bob protested. "If we do the test, and he is mine, I might consider child support, especially if we can keep this on the sly, but I'll be goddamned if I'm going to keep and raise the boy. I don't do kids."

"That's what nannies are for, numbnuts," Tiffany spat back. "Send him to an island, bustle him off to some hoity-toity English public school. I don't give a damn. I don't want a dime. I just want him off my hands."

"That's not very maternal of you, Tiffany."

"Excuse me, may I have a say in this discussion?"

Billy Bob and Tiffany turned to look at the boy, who was regarding them with what Billy Boy could only describe as scorn.

"Mother, why would you think that I'd want to live with this insincere, bible-bashing moron? He's an embarrassment, not only to himself, but to his religion."

Tiffany said, "Mikey, listen to Momma. This so-called moron makes at least two mill a year from the other morons who believe in his trash."

"Oh, I see." Mikey turned away from his mother and walked over to Billy Bob and said, "Hi Dad, when can we go home?"

Billy Bob was flummoxed. This woman could make big trouble for him. His whole empire could vanish if she made a fuss. Maybe there was some way to make his unexpected son work to his advantage.

On the flight home, Billy Bob and Mikey sat together without saying much, enjoying the perks and comforts of First Class. The kid seemed happy enough just to stare out the window. With all the other things on his mind, Billy Bob hadn't noticed before this moment that Mikey was wearing fine leather, flesh-colored gloves, at odds with the rest of his outfit, which was pure JCPenney. "Oh, great," he thought. "The kid's got some kind of skin complaint. What do you want to bet that it's an expensive one?" He asked Mikey what the problem was with his hands and the boy smiled that spooky smile again.

"I have to wear them because if I don't, people might get hurt."

"Hunh?" Billy Bob was astounded. "What do you mean 'might get hurt'? What are you talking about, boy?" On top of the skin complaint, did the kid have mental problems as well? Fabulous.

"I channel things from other things. If something bad wants to come out, then a person could get hurt, is all I'm saying. It happened when we were living in Kansas City. They nearly put me away in some prison for nutty kids. If Mom and I hadn't done a midnight flit, we'd both be in the hoosegow."

"Jesus save me, you mean you're a fugitive from justice?" Billy Bob hissed.

"Nah, they eventually dropped the charges. They couldn't prove anything. The autopsy results were inconclusive, but not every nine year old dies from a heart attack, so you could understand their concern."

Billy Bob couldn't help but pull back a bit, which was difficult considering he was strapped into an airplane seat. "What do you mean by 'channel,' anyway? Who's channeling what?"

Mikey sighed and spoke slowly, as if he was talking to a retarded child. "I don't know who or what is doing this through me. Could be aliens, angels, demons, the government, the French—it's a crapshoot. All I know is that from the moment that I could string two sentences together, I had the power of what I call 'The Touch.' Do you want to see?"

Billy Bob pulled back again, straining his seat belt and almost wishing he hadn't started the conversation. But his curiosity got the better of him. Just as Mikey was in the process of peeling off one of his gloves, the stewardess came over to ask them if they wanted any complimentary drinks or snacks. They both answered in the negative and Billy Bob waited impatiently until she moved out of earshot.

Mikey asked, "Do you want to see 'The Good Hand,' or 'The Bad Hand' first?"

"Dealer's choice, kid," Billy Bob replied.

Mikey smiled and slowly took off the glove from his left hand, his "Bad Hand," as he called it. Billy Bob had seen some messed up people in his time on the road, when his revival tent tour would dredge up some of God's more unfortunate-looking believers, who hobbled into his tent praying that Billy Bob might cure their hideous afflictions. Unfortunately, all he was really good at was giving them a smidgen of hope and taking their money. But the hand on this kid, it was something. It was evil. (Not that Billy Bob believed in evil, or even in the devil, but if anything could be described as evil, it was his son's hand.) It was nasty, shiny bluey-black and satanically insectile. Just looking at it gave him the creeps and turned his guts to ice water.

Billy Bob told Mikey to put his glove back on his "Bad Hand," toot sweet. The kid obeyed, pleased that he'd managed to freak out his dad in such a short space of time.

"Shit, boy, can't the doctors do anything about that? I mean, cutting it off would be better than walking around with that thing on the end of your arm."

"A skin specialist looked at it a couple of years ago. He disobeyed my advice not to touch it and he got a brain embolism. If it hadn't been for my 'Good Hand' and the fact we were in a hospital at the time, he'd be dead. Luckily, he's only paralyzed on his left side now."

"Damn." Billy Bob was worried. Now he realized what Tiffany was talking about when she mentioned exorcising the kid.

"Okay, let's see the other one."

Again, Mikey did a slow, smiling, striptease with his glove, revealing his "Good Hand." In many ways, Billy Bob was more frightened of this appendage. It reminded him of one of DaVinci's drawings of the hand of God, or Jesus maybe. He had a strange feeling in the pit of his stomach, like when you see a beautiful woman for the first time. The hand—and even as he was experiencing the sensations, he knew how weird it was— the hand was so perfect, so beautiful, so golden, so fine, that Billy Bob felt like he was falling in love with it. He reached out to touch it and Mikey snatched it away.

"You got to be careful. This one's more dangerous than the other one." Mikey hurriedly put his gloves back on.

"Why?" Billy Bob asked. The pain of "The Good Hand" being withdrawn was palpable. The loss was heart-breaking.

"Whatever evil 'The Bad Hand' reveals about a person's soul, 'The Good Hand' seems to have the power to put right, but sometimes it doesn't work out the way that person wants it to," Mikey said.

"Just one touch, please."

"You don't know what you're asking. I don't want to hurt you. When I figure it out, I'll let you touch it."

"Has your momma touched it?" Billy Bob said, trying, unsuccessfully it turned out, to not sound jealous.

"Of course," Mikey replied. Billy Bob's face flushed with a quick anger and a covetousness that not even he could understand. "But Mom is immune. She doesn't get hurt by 'The Bad Hand' and she can't receive any benefits from 'The Good Hand.' She's lucky."

Billy Bob gazed into his son's clear blue, guileless (or were they?) eyes. The wave of rage and jealousy had passed. This child, preternaturally intelligent, well-spoken and mature, had a gift. An idea came to Billy Bob. An idea that could make him—and his son, of course—very rich. Very, very rich.

As Billy Bob tossed and turned that night—the very same night that he and his son returned from Biloxi and settled into his mansion in a smug suburban backwater of Spokane, Washington, he wondered how this could have happened. How could a child of his turn out this way? Maybe he should have some kind of DNA test done, but what would it show on his side: that he shouldn't have gone to work as a janitor in the nuclear power plant at Hanford all those years ago? Or that he should have bypassed that stint slaving away in that pissant little gift shop in

Love Canal, New York? Of course, Billy Bob's experimentation with certain prohibited substances in his college years probably hadn't helped his over-stimulated genes either. Whatever had happened, whether it was drugs, toxic waste, or an overdose of radiation, he'd fathered some kind of mutant kid.

On the other hand, who's to say that it wasn't an "Act of God?" Not that Billy Bob believed any of that horseshit, but his devoted, deluded followers didn't need to know that. Yes, little Mikey, born of the Reverend Billy Bob Bannon, out of an illicit relationship with a fallen, Mary Magdalenesque, red-haired call girl called Tiffany—well, that sounded a hell of a lot better. And little Mikey was blessed with a talent that needed to be nurtured into something BIG. The Church of Michael the Young Redeemer and Healer. That had a nice ring to it.

It took a few months to set everything up. Billy Bob's business advisors, Deke and Stevo Highdecker, were hot for the idea, although he could tell that neither of them personally warmed to Mikey, but what did they care, as long as the cash rolled in? And shark-souled as Deke and Stevo were, they could size up the kid and scent his potential like their fishy kindred could scent blood in the water.

So, the Church of Michael the Young Redeemer and Healer opened up in a converted TV studio on Main Street in Spokane, just down from the Jehovah's Witnesses and across the way from the Buddhists' store front temple. Billy Bob had a conference with his TV people and when he revealed Mikey's "Hands of Good and Evil," they freaked out for two minutes and then immediately started to figure out how they could get enough footage for an Easter Special.

The only problem was—and Billy Bob guessed he should have known this—was the young man himself. Mikey didn't want to show his hands off to a bunch of "crazies in a church" as he put it and he certainly didn't want to "perform like a monkey" in front of TV-viewing millions. As far as Mikey was concerned, the Bible was for the birds, written by amateurs—just like Wikipedia, but without the fact-checkers. However, Billy Bob wore him down eventually, feeding his ego and intelligence, telling him that he, Mikey, could hoodwink hundreds of thousands of people into sending him money and it was all legal. Nobody could touch them, because in America, all sorts of religious stupidity were allowed.

The first *Michael the Young Redeemer and Healer Show* went out on Good Friday and Billy Bob spent days beforehand with his advisors working on his sermon. It had to be worded carefully, as Billy Bob's claims were, as far as he knew, completely without foundation. But he worked the sermon, shaped it, contorted his words, snaked around the issues and generally made up the biggest load of tosh-filled, Bible-referenced windage in the world. He was very proud. He showed it to Mikey and was pleased to see that, after his initial hilarity, even the kid had to admit it was a masterpiece.

On his end, Mikey rehearsed with a few well-chosen subjects, mostly street people gathered from alongside the railway tracks and the riverfront park. There were a few glitches along the way, but nothing that showed up in the news, or that couldn't be cured by a free bottle of Jack Daniels.

Lights. Camera. Action. Billy Bob walked out to welcome the studio audience, who were sitting comfortably in the gleaming Church-TV Studio oak-hewn pews. He spoke and his followers saw that it was good:

"My friends, if you are watching me today, you know the tenets of my ministry well. You know that I abhor all adulterers, all sinners, all fraudsters, all fakes, all bankers, all politicians, all abortionists, all gays and lesbians, all liberals, all journalists and especially all those God-denying atheists out there propagating like flies. All those who spit in the face of Our Lord. Unless they repent. Yes, if only they would be penitent. We would forgive them if they gave up their heathen wicked ways and atoned for their sins," Billy Bob said.

"My friends, you all know that for many years, I've been a lone man, fighting a losing battle against the transgressions and corruption that are infesting this nation. I've had my dark nights of the soul, as you all have. When my wife left me all those years ago, although she broke my heart, I knew that it had to be for a good reason. God's reason. For we were without issue; we could not have children. Not that I'd blame my poor, benighted, adulterous wife for that, but she did leave me for greener pastures." Billy Bob allowed a manly little sob to escape his lips.

"But I know now that it was God's will," he continued. "For I also found a green pasture to lie down in, to give me comfort unto the Lord. 'He maketh me to lie down in green pastures: he leadeth me beside the still waters.' Psalm 23:2. That soothing green pasture was a beautiful woman named Tiffany." The audience buzzed with this new revelation.

"My friends, she was a fallen woman, as Mary Magdalene was, but remember, our Lord loved Mary as he loved himself and he said: 'He that is without sin among you, let him first cast a stone at her.' John 8:7. Jesus forgave Mary Magdalene and I forgave Tiffany her sinful life, for underneath her surface corruption I could see that her soul was pure. We lay together as a married couple, even though we were not wed, but through the darkness of sin, came a light. A light of divinity, a light so bright that it blinded me when I first saw it." Billy Bob shielded his eyes dramatically as the studio audience leaned forward with anticipation.

"My son, Michael, he of the light, named after the Angel of Light, entered my life a short time ago and I now know that God saw fit to make my one night of sinfulness into something so powerful and so good, that it nearly struck me dumb. 'Fear not, for you will not be ashamed; be not confounded, for you will not be disgraced; for you will forget the shame of your youth . . .' Isaiah 54:4.

"For Michael, in whose name I have christened this new church, has been blessed through our union by God and hence he has been given a great gift directly from God. A gift that passeth all understanding. A gift that only angels could comprehend.

"Michael has the power of life and death, of good and evil, in his hands, my friends. His touch will either redeem you, it will either save you—or it will send you straight to the bowels of hell to burn for all time. It is not his decision, for his power comes directly from God. But take comfort in the fact that Michael is your ally in the fight against eternal evil. 'And there was war in heaven: Michael and his angels fought against the dragon.' Revelation 12:7.

"Michael's sole purpose in life is to be here for you. Each and every one of you. Yes, my friends, my son is prepared to sacrifice the normal, everyday life of a normal everyday child to become your savior. Remember Daniel 12:1: 'And at that time shall Michael stand up, the great prince which standeth for the children of thy people: and there shall be a time of trouble, such as never was since there was a nation *even* to that same time: and at that time thy people shall be delivered, every one that shall be found written in the book.'" Billy Bob paused dramatically, just before the last sprint to the end.

"Now, prepare to witness the miracle, the miracle of my son, the miracle of Michael the Young Redeemer and Healer!" Billy Bob shouted. "Michael is here for all those who want to be healed. All those who want to be saved. All those who seek the truth.

"Now, we just happen to have here today some willing volunteers who will be happy to test Michael's power—his God-given power. Yes, every one of these brave and strong believers in the faith will give themselves up to Michael and allow his 'Hands of Good and Evil' to decide their fate. They will literally put themselves in Michael's—and God's— 'Hands.' And remember, God moves in mysterious ways. Hallelujah!"

To thunderous applause, Mikey walked out on the stage, wearing a startling white outfit that was a carbon copy of his father's, with the addition of a pair of bejeweled gloves: one decorated with black crystals and the other one with silver. They were so blingful that Michael Jackson himself (if he'd still been alive, that is) would have coveted them. The lights picked up on the crystals and reflections danced across the studio floor, as if they were coming from two miniature mirror balls—like God's own disco.

People gasped at the sight, as both Billy Bob and Mikey had calculated his appearance very carefully for maximum effect. Mikey did look almost divine, in an over-freckly, Billy-Mumy-from-the-TV-series-*Lost-in-Space* kind of way.

Mikey mounted a specially built podium, so he appeared to be taller than his father. He took in a long, shaky breath, unaccustomed to public speaking as he was. But deep in his heart, Mikey knew he was up to the task. Showmanship was as thoroughly ingrained in his DNA as his mutated hands were. Mikey raised his arms up and spoke. The crowd and the TV audience listened with rapt attention.

"'And let the beauty of the Lord our God be upon us: and establish thou the work of our HANDS upon us; yea, the work of our HANDS establish thou it.' Psalm 90:17," Mikey intoned.

He reached over his head and ripped off the glittering glove from the "Good Hand," which Mikey then dramatically pointed up to the heavens. Everyone in the studio audience and all those watching on the box at home gasped as one. People cried and prostrated themselves in front of their television sets. It was truly the most beautiful hand in the world, especially as it was set off so artistically by the studio lighting.

Mikey continued: "Our Lord Jesus Christ said, 'Behold my HANDS, that it is I myself . . .' Luke 24:39." People in close proximity fell to their knees. The phones started ringing off the hook. Mikey was instantly hooked on the adulation.

In another dramatic gesture, he ripped off the black crystal glove covering his "Bad Hand" and then lifted both up to the ceiling, while he shouted (backed up with impressive reverb effects from the sound technician), "'Now therefore, O God, strengthen my HANDS.' Nehemiah 6:9."

A woman fainted and was almost trampled by the crowd as they surged forward towards Mikey. Luckily, Billy Bob had anticipated this and had some hunky bodyguards move in to contain the mob.

"Please, my friends," Billy Bob pleaded. "Stay back. Return to your seats. Everyone will have a chance to see."

The bodyguards shoved the crowd back to the pews. When things had quieted down, Mikey gestured for the guinea pigs to be shepherded over to him.

One man stepped forward and said, "Michael, my name is Brian and I'm a bad man. I've spent time in prison for rape. I'm no good, but I want to change, honest. Will you help me?" Mikey looked at Brian closely. He looked like a "bad'un," as his mother used to say: squinty-eyed, shabbily clothed, dirty and smelly. Mikey didn't like him, so he thought that this was the ideal man upon which to test his powers for the first time in front of the TV cameras. Mikey quietly directed Brian to turn around so he faced the audience.

Mikey raised both arms heavenwards again: "O God, strengthen my hands. Search out the evil in this man!" and then he clapped his "Bad Hand" on the top of Brian's head.

Brian shrieked with pain and surprise. Blood squirted out of his eyeballs. His knees buckled, but Pork Chop and Duffle, two of the heftiest bodyguards, were on hand to catch him and prop him up.

Mikey hollered: "'And when ye spread forth your HANDS, I will hide mine eyes from you: yea, when ye make many prayers, I will not hear: your HANDS are full of blood.' Isaiah 1:15."

Brian juddered violently, as if he was having an epileptic fit. Blood spouted from his nose, dribbled from his open, silently screaming mouth and his ears. The audience was stunned into silence, some even noticing that blood was seeping through Brian's pants in his nether regions. They thought they were going to experience a ceremony of healing, not witness a horror show.

In his previous encounters, Mikey had never felt anything untoward with his (what he truly considered) accidental victims, just a rushing, "channeling" feeling as he called it, but this time, everything seemed to work in reverse. He was receiving a barrage of images from Brian's brain: countless women being raped and murdered, their naked, brutalized bodies being disposed of like garbage—carelessly dumped in rivers and forest thickets. Mikey realized that not only was Brian a convicted rapist, he was a murderer as well—a serial killer. Mikey felt like throwing up, but he continued on:

"May the power of God compel the malicious spirits out of this corruption that is your body!" Mikey shouted.

Slumped between Pork Chop and Duffle, a stinky, drooling Brian looked a goner at this point and the same woman who had fainted earlier stood up and vomited spectacularly over the man seated in front of her.

Mikey whipped away his left hand and placed his right hand on top of Brian's head, at the same time yelling, "Brian, go forth and sin no more!" Heavenly lighting and sound effects accompanied his movements as Brian jerked upright and his mouth opened in an enormous "O" of surprise, uncannily mimicking the expression of a blow-up sex doll. Now, with a little help from the special effects technician, myriad lights were swirling around Brian, making him look like a refugee from an ancient Jefferson Airplane video. Brian gurgled some very disturbing sounds, a combination of whale song and great ape calls: "whoooo, whoooo, whoooop!"

Mikey removed his "Good Hand" and Brian shook himself free from Pork Chop and Duffle. He boogied a crazy, hopping-on-hot-coals kind of dance and hollered, "I'm saved!"

The audience went nuts, applauding frantically. Brian collapsed in a heap. Pork Chop and Duffle swiftly dragged him off to an ambulance that was waiting in the wings. White-coated janitors leapt into action, cleaning up the slug-like trail of blood on the studio floor. Billy Bob felt the teensiest little swirl of jealousy. This was truly spectacular. Billy Bob moved forward to take over the proceedings. Everyone had agreed that the first show should only have one "Purification Rite," or whatever they were going to call it.

Mikey slowly knelt down on the podium on one knee, his arms crossed over his chest in a Knights Templar pose, trying to compute the murderous show-reel that was playing over and over in his head. He stood up and looked straight at the camera and announced, "Brian has revealed his sins to me. Brian is not only a rapist, but he is a murderer as well. I witnessed his crimes. I saw his victims. Hidden away for years, they cry to me for justice. I will speak for them now."

Billy Bob's jaw dropped. This hadn't happened during rehearsals. The other guinea pigs looked uncomfortable. What hidden miserable secrets could Michael winnow out from their hearts? Michael raised his arms again and this time a woman frantically ran towards him. "My name is Eileen and I've been told over and over that I am a sinner. Michael, can you seek out the truth within me?" she cried.

Mikey was tired, drained, with the thoughts of a serial killer rampaging through his brain, but, in spite of his mental exhaustion, he gestured to Pork Chop and Duffle, who moved into position. Billy Bob felt like his show was being hijacked, but the crowd was baying for more and he might cause more of a ruckus by stopping the proceedings than by letting them continue.

Mikey's left hand descended upon the woman's head and images of Eileen's sad and pathetic life flooded into his consciousness. Mikey didn't know much, or even care about the reasons why women have abortions. In his mother's more cruelly drunken moments, she'd tell him straight out how she wished that she'd gotten rid of Mikey before he'd grown into the problem child that he was. But Eileen's stupidity and ignorance had caused her to have three abortions. Yet, all her regret at terminating her children hadn't stopped her from having yet another unfortunate, unprotected liaison with some no-hope, pizza-brained guy who'd left her in the lurch.

However, Mikey's true feelings about abortion and their moral convolutions did not concern him, because what was flowing from Eileen was not her remorse, or sadness, but the angry, howling, unbearable screams of the unborn fetuses, demanding retribution. The rage flooded Mikey's brain and he was almost knocked backwards with the force of it.

Between the furious fetuses, the naked dead women and the twisted faces of Brian and Eileen filling his head, Mikey was feeling pretty wretched.

He opened his eyes and that's when he noticed the noise. He looked down from the podium at Eileen, her head lolling back, her bleeding eyes looking into his, pleading for him to make it stop. He whipped his left hand off the top of her head and then laid on his right hand, hoping to channel some good into this ghastly woman. Eileen jerked and jumped straight up into the air as soon as Mikey made contact, then fell down on the ground in a steaming heap. Pork Chop whisked her up in his arms and hurried for the ambulance.

The audience was again dumbstruck. What was this kid doing to these people, cooking their brains like popcorn? Was he a healer, or just a dangerous freak?

Mikey looked into the camera again: "The sad truth about Eileen is that although she is a good person, her ignorance put her at odds with the new hopeful lives that grew within her. Her lost children scream to me. I speak for them. I speak for the dead. They are crying in the wilderness."

Mikey raised his arms again and Billy Bob noticed with a stab of horror that the insectile blackness of Mikey's "Bad Hand" was creeping up his arm almost to his elbow. The attractiveness of his "Good Hand" was diminishing: not so golden, not so compelling. The evil (and now Billy Bob believed in it, oh yes) was growing and the good retreating. And at what cost to his son?

Mikey had sunk back down into his Knights Templar pose. The woman who had fainted and vomited before now began to scream and Billy Bob decided that the insanity must cease. He signaled the bodyguards to slowly clear the audience out of the studio.

Billy Bob walked to the front of the podium and said, "My friends, today you saw two miracles. I must admit, I didn't know what to expect, certainly not this. But Michael is compelled to do the Lord's work and that is what he has done. He has transmogrified the evil in people's souls into something good.

"Michael needs your help, so please send five dollars or more for his ministry today without delay, to the address that you can see right now on your TV screens, so he can help more sinners. Thank you and God Bless."

Billy Bob didn't see Mikey rise up behind him. He had removed his white linen jacket and ripped off his shirt, showing his thin boyish freckled chest. Mikey raised his arms again. The creeping darkness was now visibly slithering up Mikey's left arm and across his upper torso. Thin tendrils curled up his neck, creating a Maori-like tattoo effect, which soon took over his face. This was no CGI, no magic from the lighting guy. This was really happening.

Mikey opened his mouth and stuck his tongue out: a pointed, lizard-like, bile green horror. It was at this precise moment that Billy Bob turned around to take in the sight of his blackened, wasted, ruined son, whose frail body now contained the evil remnants of Brian's crimes and the wrath of Eileen's unborn children. Mikey's bloodshot eyes met Billy Bob's baby blues and Billy Bob realized too late that his fabulous idea of capitalizing on his son's "talent" was a big mistake.

But Mikey was a survivor. Deep down in the reptilian part of his brain (the eat-shit-fight-fuck part), something was stirring. He needed to live on, to continue his work, so Mikey did what most animals do when they ingest something poisonous: he vomited. But it wasn't just a polite little retch; it was a colossal projectile vomit that would have entered the *Guinness World Records*, if there were an entry for such a thing. And Mikey's power puke was so vile, so noxious, so putrid that the flow, when it hit the unfortunate Billy Bob full in the face, was a lethal cocktail that burned and blinded him in an instant.

Billy Bob dropped to the floor, writhing and howling in agony. Everyone in the studio was screaming, but Mikey didn't stop. The rancid turgid blackness continued to gush from his mouth and other people were hit. They also fell shrieking to the ground, as if burned by acid. Pandemonium and fear gripped the crowd.

If it hadn't been for the bravery of Pork Chop and Duffle, it would have been an even bigger bloodbath than it actually turned out to be. From either side of the soundstage, they sprinted up to the podium, tackled Mikey and brought him down to the floor. However, Mikey continued to spew out his evil vomit of death. Pork Chop—having served in the Special Forces—instantly accessed the danger and took action, realizing that it was a "him or us" situation. He put Mikey's noggin in a headlock and then wrenched it sharply to the right, hearing the telltale "click" of a neck being broken. The geyser of horror stopped, but Pork Chop could have sworn he heard a child's voice whispering in his ear, "You can't kill me."

"Did you hear that?" a startled Pork Chop said to Duffle, but Duffle was already up on his feet and moving to Billy Bob's side. Pork Chop turned back to look into Mikey's staring, glassy eyes. He knew the kid had to be dead. The evil darkness was already fading from Mikey's face.

Duffle turned Billy Bob over. His face was burned beyond recognition and the insufferable pain had caused a massive coronary. Billy Bob was well on his way to meet his Maker.

Duffle was a man of few words, but he knew his Bible. He turned to the jostling crowd and the TV cameras, and announced: "But of the tree of the knowledge of good and evil, thou shalt not eat of it: for in the day that thou eatest thereof thou shalt surely die.' Genesis 2:17."

The remaining audience dropped to their knees as one and cried, "Amen!" Duffle was a bit surprised and gratified. What power do words possess!

After he recovered, Brian happily confessed to all his crimes. He was extradited to a Red State and summarily executed. He had a smile on his face when the lethal injection finally hit his blood stream. Eileen joined a convent and became renowned as a talented singer-songwriter in the "Singing Nun" mode.

Pork Chop and Duffle managed to avoid any charges in the Mikey affair and started up a ministry of their own.

Billy Bob and Mikey were buried in Spokane's Riverside Memorial Park cemetery side by side. Tiffany came to pay her respects and wept, wondering if she'd only kept her mouth shut maybe both her boys would still be alive. But being a hard-bitten broad, she was soon over it and bellying up to the bar at the nearby Riverside Tavern for a few comforting margaritas.

Later that night, after all the grave diggers had gone home, the dirt shifted above Mikey's grave, as if some powerful creature was trying to free himself from his boxy prison. The next day, Harvey Mention, the cemetery gardener, was astounded to see that Mikey's grave had been opened and desecrated: the coffin empty, the body gone.

Harvey thought he could hear a boyish voice murmuring from the shadows: "And the Lord God said, 'Behold, the man is become as one of us, to know good and evil: and . . . he put forth his HAND, and take also of the tree of life, and eat, and live for ever.' Genesis 3:22."

THE ALPDRÜCKE

"Sleep Tight and Don't Let the Demons Bite!"

"**P**OCK!"

The noise startled Jim awake. He opened his eyes and it was deathly dark, with just a hint of moonlight coming in through the curtained windows. The high-ceilinged room was unfamiliar, bluish and vast. Gripped by fear, he could barely breathe. Then there was the sound of a ball slow bouncing towards him.

"Pock!"

Where the hell was that noise coming from? Then he heard a monstrous "thwack!" of something hitting the wall above his head. Ricochet . . . followed by the bouncing sound.

He tried to get up, but he was frozen, unable to move, incapable of protecting himself from whatever was toying with him. In the left-hand, logical side of his brain, he knew it must be some kind of nightmarish sleep paralysis, a complaint that he'd been suffering from for the last couple of weeks, but it didn't stop the horror of knowing that there was something in the room with him.

"Pock!"

He finally recognized the sound as a tennis racket hitting a ball. Then a "thwack!" above his head again—the ball smashing against the headboard at great velocity. The slow bouncing sound. Whoever, or whatever, was lobbing the ball at him was coming closer, he could sense it.

His breathing became frantic. He had to wake up, but it was impossible. Then, through the gloom, he perceived a darker darkness moving towards him. For the first time, he could see the luminous green ball being tossed up and then a tennis racket whooshing through the air.

"Pock!"

The brutalizer zoomed directly at his head, but at the last minute it veered up and hit the headboard again. He was hyperventilating now—moaning with fear. The figure scurried to the foot of the bed—raising up the racket once more—and that's when Jim caught sight of the strings gleaming in the moonlight. Strings made of cheese-wire, sharp as hell. He knew in his gut that if the racket made contact with his face, it would be cubed into a hundred bloody pieces.

Jim tried to scream out loud, but the only noise he could make was a girlish, high-pitched wheezing. That's when he sensed a cockroach on his pillow at ear level, tickling his earlobe with its antennae, screeching in a tinny, David-Hedison-as-*The-Fly*-caught-in-the-spider-web voice: "Wake up, wake up!"

The small figure of darker than darkness was at his bedside now. The horrifying thing was that even standing up, it was tiny. Was it some kind of satanic child perhaps? A mad, diseased ape? That concept was much worse than a grown-up monster. What was even stranger was that it seemed to be wearing some kind of ludicrous hat. However, instead of making Jim laugh, it only heightened his terror.

Suddenly, it jumped up and landed on his chest. He couldn't breathe. The gleaming racket was hovering just over his face—the blood from some previous unfortunate victim dripping off the glistening cheese wire strings—and the most hideous aspect of something peering through the racket, as if the thing was checking its reflection in a hand mirror. A glimpse of a demonic, grinning face floating above him.

Then the creature rasped: "Anyone for tennis?"

Jim finally managed to scream.

The demon's hand gripped his shoulder and shook him, as if to rouse him from his trance, so he could experience the true nastiness of his impending diced death, but then the pillow cockroach squeaked "wake up!" so loudly in his ear that real life came thundering back.

Bam! He was awake: heart racing; legs jumping; flesh goose-bumped and ice-cold; gasping for air like a dying goldfish. Marney, his girlfriend, was shaking him awake.

"Jesus, I thought you were dying," Marney said, in not a very friendly manner.

"I thought I was," wheezed Jim.

"I couldn't wake you up. Do you know how scary that is!?" Marney demanded and Jim tried to be sympathetic and failed. She attempted to pry his dream out of him, and he finally spilled the beans on the recurrent nightmare that had been keeping them both awake.

Marney said, "You're joking, right? A tennis-playing, silly hat-wearing dwarf? That's the thing that's been terrifying you for the last few weeks? Why don't you just get out of bed and squish him for goodness' sake."

Jim sighed. He was too tired to reply. Marney turned around and eventually grumbled herself back to sleep, while he lay awake, afraid to return to that unpleasant dreamland where he was so vulnerable. Eventually though, a groggy tiredness dragged him down to the pit of unconsciousness like a quagmire of quicksand and he was helpless to stop it.

He was in a deep, crystal clear, natural pool in the jungle that looked like one of those Mayan sacrificial wells where they used to gaily toss in their virgins—trying to ward off whatever fate that had eventually destroyed their civilization. A shaft of moonlight pierced the water and he could see he was at least 20 feet below the surface. He looked down and it was as if he was poised at the edge of an abyss filled with cold, black, oily water. He started to swim upwards. His heart began to race again and he was fearful that he wouldn't have enough breath to get to the top. He glanced down and that's when he saw them: white shapely arms floating up out of the depths like sea snakes beckoning to him, trying to grab his legs and drag him back down to oblivion.

He screamed and the air bubbled out of his mouth. He was drowning. The ghostly arms of a thousand dead maidens drifted up, grabbed him and held him in place.

"Pock!"

Sailing through the water was another nightmare luminous green tennis ball—zeroing in at his head. The evil dark dwarf thing had followed him here to the inky pool. He frantically thrashed his limbs to free himself from the wraithlike arms and managed to make his way up to the surface, his lungs bursting.

The wet cockroach hanging onto his shoulder for dear life shrieked in his ear: "Wake up, damn you!"

"Oh, fuck," Jim shuddered and sat up. No more sleep for him tonight.

"That's it!" Marney said. "You're going to see a doctor about this, or I'm moving out."

Jim was still trembling from the after-effects of his dream. "What's the point? It's just a dream. It's not like they can crawl into my head and slay the monster."

"Well, maybe they can give you some drugs so you can sleep. You've got to do something. You're going to have a heart attack one night if this keeps going on."

For once, Jim agreed with her.

A few days later, he was sitting in Dr Gardner's office, where he was getting the lowdown on attending a sleep clinic. Although the doctor was pretty sure that Jim was suffering from sleep paralysis—in particular, the more uncommon Recurrent Isolated Sleep Paralysis (RISP)—he felt that it was best to confirm the diagnosis by performing a multi-parametric test at a sleep clinic.

Called a Polysomnography (PSG), the test would make a comprehensive recording of the biophysiological changes that occur during sleep. The PSG would monitor many of Jim's body functions including the brain (EEG), eye movements (EOG), muscle activity or skeletal muscle activation (EMG) and heart rhythm (ECG) during sleep. The clinic's technicians would also monitor respiratory airflow and respiratory effort, along with peripheral pulse oximetry (the saturation of Jim's hemoglobin).

How the hell Jim was supposed to sleep with gizmos stuck on his head, chest and fingers, as well as up his nose was beyond him. On the other hand, perhaps all those distractions might keep his death dwarf from bothering him.

It was just a few hours before his appointment and Jim went to the local café to calm his nerves and try to finish the graphic novel he was struggling to design. Lack of sleep was making his creative life a mess. The waitress brought over his usual order of a decaf black coffee and apple pie, and he was about to tuck in when a hand descended on his shoulder. Jim nearly jumped out of his socks, but it was just Marney, on a cigarette break from her law office around the corner. There was someone with her, a tall, distinguished-looking, older man with twinkling blue eyes and a heavy German accent. He looked a little bit like the alien guy, Klaatu, from the original 1951 version of *The Day the Earth Stood Still*, except his strong eyebrows, as black as his hair was white, met in the middle. She introduced him as Mr. Zeiner, a friend of hers from the accounting department of her law firm.

They both sat down at his table and Jim wondered why Zeiner had joined them.

Marney: "Jim, I've been chatting to Mr. Zeiner about your sleep paralysis. He thinks he may know what's bothering you."

Jim was baffled and annoyed, but he didn't show it. He hated it when Marney talked to strangers about his problems.

Jim: "Listen, I'm visiting the sleep clinic tonight. Until I get the telemetry, no one's going to know what the diagnosis really is. Unless Mr. Zeiner here is a doctor?"

Mr. Zeiner: "No, my young friend, I am not a doctor. However, I am familiar with these demons of the night."

Jim: "Whoa, buddy. I suffer from nightmares and sleep paralysis. That's it."

Mr. Zeiner: "Nightmares cannot possibly explain the extreme terrors you are experiencing. Tell me, have you ever been to Germany?"

Jim: "No."

Mr. Zeiner: "You see, the fact that your demon dwarf wore a hat is very significant. It serves as his cloak of invisibility, if you like. This particular demon is called an Alp and it is very well known in Germanic folklore. What you experienced was an Alpdrücke, an 'Alp attack,' where an Alp jumps on your chest and tries to suffocate you. You are very lucky that it did not try to suck blood from your nipples as well, or even strangle you. As for the tennis racket . . ."

Jim: ". . . sorry, I gotta go to the john."

Jim got up from the table and walked briskly to the toilets, rapidly followed by Marney. She grabbed his arm and he shook her off.

Marney: "Don't be so rude! He's only trying to help."

Jim: "You're joking, right?"

Marney: "Mr. Zeiner says that he's come across a lot of these cases in Germany. He thinks he can help you."

Jim: "You know, Marney, I think I'll leave myself to the ministrations of science, thank you very much. Tell Mr. Zeiner that I had to leave because I had an appointment with my local exorcist, okay?"

Jim left through the side entrance, the steam almost visibly coming out of his ears. Was Marney crazy? What was she thinking of?

A few hours later, Jim was lying in a bed in the Eastside Sleep Clinic. The pillow was comfy enough and the sheets clean and sweet smelling. The clinic technicians had wired him up so they could monitor his EEG, EOG, EMG and ECG. They placed a pulse oximeter on his finger and put pressure transducers in his nose to measure his nasal airflow. He stared at the ceiling, trying to relax, trying to forget Marney and stupid old Mr. Zeiner, with his tales of Germanic demons with crazy hats.

In forty minutes, Jim had achieved the first level of NREM (Non-Rapid Eye Movement—sleep) called Stage N1. This occurred mostly in the beginning of sleep, accompanied by slow eye movements. The alpha waves disappeared and the theta wave appeared. People aroused from this stage often believe that they have been fully awake.

Then he slipped into Stage 2, when no eye movement occurs and dreaming is very rare.

At Stage 3, Jim reached deep, slow-wave sleep. Delta waves began to occur and then dominated. Dreaming was more common in this stage than in other stages of NREM sleep. The content of dreams during this stage tended to be disconnected, less vivid, and less memorable than those that occurred during REM sleep.

Finally, Jim settled into REM (Rapid Eye Movement) sleep, characterized by the rapid and random movement of the eyes. The activity of the brain's neurons was quite similar to that during waking hours and the sleeper was more likely to remember dreams from this stage.

The technicians, Brad Durning and Samantha Pesce (also known as Sam), were keeping an eye on Jim's polysomnography recordings in the monitor room, which was filled with banks of computers and monitor screens. They were having a coffee break when Samantha saw something out of the corner of her eye scurrying around Jim's small bedroom.

"What the fuck is that?" Sam stood up and exclaimed, nearly spilling her coffee on the console—rather unprofessional behavior in Brad's opinion.

"What?" he replied and then she pointed at the CCTV monitor linked to Jim's room.

"Whoah, is that a rat?" Brad said, halfway out of his chair, as the thing, whatever it was, scampered under Jim's bed.

At the same time, Sam noticed that Jim was in distress, making the high-pitched whimpering noises that Marney had reported to the technicians in the initial conference stage of the diagnosis. His heart rate was also up and his EEG was spiking—showing high levels of mental activity.

Brad jumped up and ran to Jim's room, reluctantly followed by Sam. Arriving at the door, he turned the knob, but for some unfathomable reason, it didn't work. He turned around to a panting Sam, who had just arrived.

"These doors can't lock from the inside, can they?" he asked, already knowing the answer.

"These doors can't be locked at all. It must be stuck," she replied.

Brad turned the knob again and shoved his shoulder up against the door, but no luck.

In the clinic bedroom, Jim was lying helpless as the dream dwarf leapt on his chest. It unbuttoned his pajama top and playfully tweaked his nipples before casually leaning down and viciously biting them until blood came. It started to lap delicately at the blood with its tongue. Jim overcame his terror and screamed as loud as he could.

Outside in the corridor, Brad took a few steps back and then hurled himself at the door. It flew open and he tumbled into the darkened room. Sam followed to give him moral support. And then the door slammed behind them.

In the monitor room, while all the machines beeped quietly, the only sounds coming from Jim's CCTV audio were the whistling of a tennis racket swooshing through the air, followed by the "Pock!" of balls being violently smacked. Then the screaming began.

Two hours later, Doug Sampson and Brenda Forge, Brad and Sam's 4 a.m. relief, came into the ominously quiet monitor room. They looked around and spotted the images on Jim's CCTV monitor. His room was still dimly lit, but the light from the hallway spilled into the room. They could see two figures lying on the floor, surrounded by puddles of dark liquid. Brenda didn't hesitate and called security and the police, while Doug cautiously walked down the corridor to Jim's room.

Blood was creeping out of the doorway across the corridor floor. Doug stayed there and looked in, then warily put his hand around the doorframe to turn on the bedroom's light switch. When he caught a glimpse of what was lying on the floor, his medical training deserted him. He whirled around and threw up spectacularly all over the corridor walls.

Gobs of gore and brains were splattered Jackson Pollock-like across the bedroom walls and floor. Brad and Sam were dead: their white uniforms drenched in blood; their faces gruesomely cubed into hundreds of pieces, as if some demon from hell had prepared an obscene feast of face cubes instead of the usual cheese cubes for a satanic cocktail party. All that was missing were the toothpicks.

Jim, on the other hand, was sleeping peacefully on the bed; the only sign of mayhem was the blood from a couple of wounds on his chest. Somehow he had escaped the slaughter.

Marney sat in the office of homicide detective Jason Strummer, nervously wondering how on earth this could have happened. Jim was in a holding cell—still in his pajamas—protesting his innocence. It was hard to imagine how Jim of all people could have murdered the two sleep clinic technicians.

Detective Strummer entered the room, a DVD in his hand. He looked at Marney appreciatively: blonde hair, great tits, long athletic legs. He wondered how the lanky, nervous bozo in Holding Cell 9 could have nabbed such a beauty, but hey, there's no accounting for taste in the world.

"Looks like we're going to have to let your boyfriend go," he said as he sat down behind his desk and Marney's face brightened.

"I told you Jim couldn't have done such a thing," she scolded.

"We looked at the CCTV recordings and Jim was in bed the whole time during the attacks. It's very weird. Here were two people running around the room, yelling their heads off, pounding on a door that can't be locked and there's your boyfriend lying there dead asleep."

"So who murdered those poor people?" asked Marney.

"That's the problem. We can't see who killed them. The victims are either blocking the camera at the wrong time, or something unidentified moves between them and the camera. We can see the damage being inflicted on both of the victims, but we can't see the perp. It's bizarre.

"We also rewound the recording back to the point where we could see something scuttling around Jim's room—the incident that must have prompted the victims to go check on Jim in the first place—but again the images are too fuzzy to make any firm deductions on what it could be."

"What about Jim's wounds?"

"Well, it certainly looks like something bit him. We just don't know what. We're getting the bite marks analyzed, but nothing so far. But the blood on his chest is definitely his, not the technicians'."

"So Jim is free to go now?"

"Yeah, but tell him not to leave town. Whether he was conscious or not, he's a material witness to a double homicide."

It was Zeiner's show now.

Jim couldn't science his way out of meeting up with the old guy, because Marney was threatening to move out if he didn't. According to Zeiner, the fact that the creature bit Jim's nipples and sucked his blood was a dead giveaway that the perpetrator was an Alp and Jim was too damn exhausted to argue.

Zeiner came over to their place a week after the disastrous incident at the clinic. His plan was to monitor Jim's sleep, sitting in a chair in their bedroom, while Marney slept in the spare room. Zeiner had brought all sorts of traditional accruements to assist him in his exorcism of the Alp. These included favorite Alp repellents such as a broomstick to lay under Jim and Marney's bed; iron horseshoes to hang from the bedpost; a mirror to place on Jim's chest and a large silver cross to hang on the headboard. Then Zeiner plugged the keyhole in the bedroom door, a common method of entry for Alps. Jim also had to sleep with a nightlight, as this was another effective way to ward off an Alpdrücke.

Marney retired for the night and Jim tried to get to sleep, but he was a bit weirded out by Zeiner's presence in the room. Jim peeked through a nearly closed eyelid and the old guy was staring at him in a particularly unnerving fashion. Jim tried to turn over, but the mirror got in his way.

"I can't sleep with this thing on my chest," Jim complained.

"Would you rather have an Alp sitting on your chest, with his infernal tennis racket?" asked Zeiner.

"Hey, that's right. You were going to tell me about the tennis racket," said Jim.

"It's too late now. I will in the morning," Zeiner said.

"I want to know now," Jim demanded.

"All right, my impatient friend. It is an unusual implement, to be sure, but Alps are mischievous creatures. This one obviously admires the game of tennis, so in his twisted way, he finds it amusing to "slice and dice" (as you Americans say) his victims using a tennis racket strung with cheese wire. And the balls he uses are interesting. It makes you wonder what they are made of—to be so resistant against cheese wire."

"Teflon, maybe?" Jim asked sarcastically.

Zeiner ignored him and continued, "Normally, Alps are not so vicious, so this is a very unusual occurrence. It is possible that this Alp is not necessarily a demon, but a particularly unpleasant human. After death, his unquiet spirit metamorphosed into an Alp. So perhaps this Alp in his previous human existence was a tennis player? Who knows?" Zeiner pontificated.

"What a load of bilge," Jim mumbled and closed his eyes.

4 a.m., the darkest hour. The time when humans have their most tenuous hold on life—their most fragile grip on the planet. Jim knew in his heart that all the precautions Zeiner had taken were inadequate. The Alp was coming to get him.

Jim's feelings of anxiety were at their height and not only for his own sake. He wondered if Zeiner was going to get butchered by the Alp. Having already been a suspect from the previous clinic carnage, albeit briefly, the police would definitely try to pin Zeiner's murder on him for sure.

Jim opened his eyes and he was surprised to see that he was in his own bedroom, not the vast blue room. He looked around and Zeiner was gone. What the fuck? He was supposed to be watching over him.

Jim removed the mirror from his chest and cautiously got up. He looked around: in the closet, even under the bed, and he was relieved that he couldn't find any cubed remains of Zeiner. Maybe the old bastard just needed a bathroom break.

Then Jim heard something. A moaning sound. The hairs stiffened at the back of his neck. Instead of exasperation, he felt sudden nauseous fear in the pit of his belly.

He quietly walked across the room, opened the door and peered into the hallway. It was dark, lit only by a small wall socket nightlight under the table at the end of the corridor by the bathroom. The bathroom door was open and the room beyond it dark, so Jim's theory about the old geezer taking a leak flew out the window.

Then he heard the sound again. It was coming from the spare bedroom. Where Marney was.

Now it was Marney who was trapped in the vast, blue, high-ceilinged room—moonlight splashing across her bed like a spotlight. Although she instinctively knew where she was, she had her eyes tightly shut. It was almost an out-of-body experience. In her mind's eye, she could see everything that was happening in the room from above. Marney was dreaming, but not dreaming—hovering somewhere between wakefulness and nightmare. She was helpless, unable to move, totally incapable of defending herself. She tried to call out to Jim, but every time she managed to vocalize, a hairy palm clamped itself over her nose and mouth, cutting off her air supply. She stopped and the hand was removed.

Marney was terrified, but aroused at the same time. Her nightdress was open to the waist and something was lying on top of her—biting and sucking her nipples.

Marney was too petrified to open her eyes to find out what was lying on top of her. It couldn't be the Alp, as the creature's noises of passion were not accompanied by any tennis racket sound effects. It was at her neck now, breathing heavily, then a tongue forced itself into her ear. The creature pushed her quivering legs apart. A pause while it adjusted itself, and then something hard thrust inside her.

Marney tried to scream, but the hairy hand covered her nose and mouth again. She struggled and attempted to push the thing off, but she was slowly descending into unconsciousness. She decided to take a quick peak at her attacker and was confronted by piercing blue eyes and a very recognizable black monobrow. That's when Marney knew that Jim had never been part of the plan. She had always been the target.

Marney mercifully blacked out. The Alp completed its task in record demon time and then hopped down from the bed, fully resuming its Zeiner human shape. He felt her pulse. It was still strong, even after her ordeal. He had chosen his bride well.

Zeiner tiptoed over to the door and opened it, totally unprepared to find a furious Jim standing in the hallway holding a baseball bat.

"What the fuck are you doing in Marney's room, you fucking pervert!" Jim shouted and he swung the bat at Zeiner's head. Zeiner ducked dexterously and then feinted to the left. As Jim moved in to take another swing, Zeiner shot to his right and dashed into the hallway. Jim turned to chase after him, but Zeiner had disappeared down the stairs.

Jim followed, turning on all the lights. Even though the front door was still closed and locked, and although he searched every room, including the basement, he couldn't find Zeiner.

His rage abated and Jim realized that he had no idea how long Zeiner had been in Marney's room. He ran up the stairs to find her standing in the doorway, trembling and crying. He tried to get an explanation, but she was incoherent and in shock. He bundled her into bed and called the police.

Marney never told anyone what really happened that night. She wouldn't allow a physical exam. She said that Zeiner had tried to attack her while she was sleeping and she had fought him off. She knew in her heart that it was completely illogical not to report the actual assault, but she was unable to verbalize what had happened to her. It was as if some other-worldly force had sealed her lips on the subject. Or maybe it was just a dream after all?

Zeiner didn't show up at work the next day. His address was found to be an old warehouse downtown that hadn't been used in years. He had simply disappeared. Along with Jim's sleep paralysis.

Nine months later, Jim and Marney had a baby boy they called Jim Junior. The baby looked and acted normal (no sign of twinkling blue eyes, a German accent, or a monobrow) and Marney was mightily re-lieved.

But one day, when Jim Junior was still learning to speak, he turned to her with a wide, gummy, baby smile and, with spine-chilling clarity, spoke his first complete sentence:

"Anyone for tennis?"

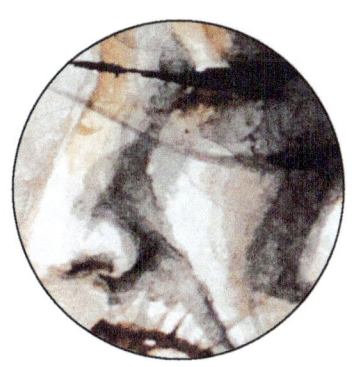

VALESKA

Chinese proverb: 一滴精, 十滴血
pinyin: yì dī jīng, shí dī xuè
"A drop of semen is equal to ten drops of blood"

VALESKA'S COLD BLUE EYES OPENED AT PRECISELY NINE O'CLOCK IN the evening. She always knew what time it was, clock or no clock. The room was dark, but she could see every detail, night vision one of the more helpful traits of being a Seminal. She rose from her bed, went into the bathroom and performed her ablutions in the same way that she did every night: sensually, taking her time, enjoying the feeling of the water on her skin, her hands massaging her body. She put on her makeup carefully, for maximum effect. Afterwards, she examined herself in the mirror and was satisfied that she looked as appetizing to the male human animal as she ever could.

She dressed provocatively in a skintight, crimson cocktail dress, with stockings, garter belt and no bra or panties. She put her black hair up in a wild, punk-style ponytail on the top of her head. She looked like a party girl on the make, ready for fun—not a predator looking for sustenance. The last thing she slipped on were her black, unborn calf's leather gloves—no grain, so they felt like human skin.

Valeska was ready to leave at eleven o'clock. Before she opened her front door, she looked through the peephole and then listened intently, to make sure that no one else was in the hallway. She hated people knowing her comings and goings. She was sure that she caused enough comment by avoiding going out during the day, but she'd be damned if she gave her nosy neighbors anything more to gossip about.

She exited her apartment and took the stairs down three floors. She left by the back service entrance, entering an alleyway that most sensible people would avoid like the plague. Valeska didn't care. She had dealt with street people and muggers before, easy prey. Too weak, or stupid, or unprepared to deal with her strength and purpose. But Valeska had standards and she avoided seeking out these kinds of targets. Her sense of smell was very acute and most of those losers stank of booze, BO, excrement or cigarettes.

Also, because she didn't want to have any personal contact with such trash, she would have to kill them first and she didn't like taking the fluid from the dead. It didn't have the same buzz of energy to it and extracting it was more trouble than it was worth. Although disease wasn't a problem for her, she was still fussy in a catlike way about her victims. She had enough problems dealing with the normal, run-of-the-mill specimens, but preying on the weak, ugly and nasty ones just added to her feelings of revulsion about the whole species.

Valeska spotted her prey almost as soon as she entered the trendy nightspot where she often went hunting. He was perfect for her. Handsome, powerful body, clean looking, and well dressed. He had an aura of prosperity about him and a smugness that came from being either a lawyer or a stockbroker. In other words, he wouldn't be missed.

After Valeska had selected her man, she put out her scent for him, a special perfume that emanated from her vagina. She aimed directly at him, so no other males could be contaminated. He was at the bar, talking to a blonde, when it hit him. He spun around in an almost comical manner and spotted her. He didn't bother to apologize to the blonde, but made a beeline over to Valeska, who was waiting patiently for him, holding an untouched vodka martini in her hand.

He was captivated, as they all were. They made meaningless small talk, but he couldn't wait to take her home with him. It was almost getting too easy to pick up men, but she didn't care. She was hungry.

They grabbed a cab back to his place, a two-story warehouse apartment in a newly gentrified part of town. Valeska studiously looked away from the CCTV cameras as they entered the lobby of his building. His apartment was very impressive, but soulless. Ridiculous modern conceptual art on the white walls. Nice parquet floor covered with uncomfortable-looking furniture. It was the opposite of her cozy apartment, with its original fixtures and baroque touches.

His name was Philip. He made them a couple of Grey Goose martinis and invited her to sit on the sofa. He sat down, but she remained standing. He looked up, puzzled, then a wide grin cracked his face as Valeska put her drink down and in one graceful movement, whisked her dress over her head. Philip laughed and she joined him, but their motivations for merriment were quite different. She took the drink from his hand and placed it on the unpleasantly angular glass coffee table. Smiling sensually, she slowly undid his belt and unzipped his pants. He helped her eagerly. Soon his Calvin Kleins and pants were puddled around his shoes. She removed his tie and he was so excited he ripped his shirt off. She knelt in front of him and caressed his arms, chest and legs; slowly massaging her way to his penis. He slouched back into the couch and she leaned over and began to suck.

At first, Valeska did it the human way, to get him in the mood and allay suspicion. He was responding well. He moaned with pleasure and gently placed his hands on either side of her head, mumbling little encouragements under his breath. She playfully used her tongue and worked on him for at least ten minutes. He tried to pull her up so he could enter her, but she begged him to let her continue on in her oral way. He shrugged and smiled and relaxed back. She then gently massaged the area just behind his penis with her gloved fingers, moving slowly towards to his anus. Philip got really excited then. She knew that he was going to come any minute. She stopped and said, "Come in my mouth, I love it, come in my mouth." He groaned and shot his load—and that's when she had him.

She changed tactics and sucked his cock again, but this time it was with her Seminal Strength. He cried out in shock and his body spasmed. What was going on? What was happening to him? But it was too late. As soon as she had got the first taste of his semen in her mouth, Philip was a goner.

He nearly blacked out with the intensity of new sensations: an almost cosmic pleasure; a hollow pain in his pelvis as if his very being was being sucked out; and a growing lethargy. Whatever was being taken from him was being substituted by some kind of opiate. He wanted to struggle, to throw the woman off, but he was too weak. He could do nothing but sit there and feel the essence of his life draining away.

Valeska stopped suddenly. She stood up and looked at him. Even in his half-dead, paralyzed state, Philip admired her magnificent body, thighs like a dancer, perfect breasts, tiny waist. Even though he knew he was going to die, he worshipped her for her beauty and her power.

Valeska smiled. She saw the adoration in his eyes. She could hear him breathing his last, quick gasps. She straddled him and gently lowered herself on his still hard penis. Philip couldn't believe it. What was this creature? Why was she doing this to him? Valeska became more excited. In these circumstances, she could come very quickly, especially with a human's new energy inside her. He came again, for the final time, which sparked Valeska's powerful unworldly orgasm. The power of her Seminal vagina now came into play. Her internal muscles contracted and drew out every last bit of semen and life essence from him. He had just enough energy to moan, but it was quickly stifled by Valeska's eager tongue thrusting deep in his mouth.

Philip died but his penis remained hard because of the process. She continued on, having multiple orgasms for at least twenty minutes afterwards. She never cried out, just silent screams of pleasure.

A very satisfying meal, it had to be said. Necrophilia is so good for the soul, even if you don't have one.

Afterwards, Valeska rested for a little while, but as soon as she stood, she was all business again. She had to clean up and be out of the apartment as soon as possible. This urgency was practical, the longer she stayed at the scene of a Feed, the chance of capture was greater. She removed some soft absorbent cloths from a ziplock bag in her purse. They had been pre-soaked in bleach to destroy any trace of DNA at the scene. She replaced her leather gloves with surgical ones and then went to work with a supernatural speed: vacuuming the living room, washing their glasses, wiping down any surfaces that her skin may have come in contact with, including the rug where she had knelt down to consume her evening meal. Her last job was to wipe the human down with the bleach-soaked cloths, paying special attention to his penis and the inside of his mouth.

All the used cloths were placed back in the ziplock bag. She didn't trust the toilet to flush down evidence. Things could always get stuck or come back up. Valeska would leave nothing for the police to find.

After she finished cleaning up, she got dressed and had a last look around. She went back to her victim's body to admire her handiwork. Philip still looked very handsome and virile, a perfect vessel for her feast.

When she left Philip's apartment, Valeska used the same routine as she did to leave her own: carefully looking out the peephole and listening for a long time, before opening the door. She had already noted the exit to the stairs. She walked down the five flights briskly, with a new energy.

She went all the way down to the basement and found the back door, avoiding the security cameras. She was soon out on the street, breathing the tainted, moist air of the city. It was raining, which pleased her. Valeska liked walking in the rain. It cooled her off and calmed her mind. She started strolling back to her apartment. She never took cabs in these circumstances.

Ten minutes later, Valeska sensed a presence behind her. Not human. Definitely someone like her. She directed her vaginal scent to him, a little friendly warning to back off. He still followed, which annoyed her. The last thing she wanted to do was to talk shop. She needed to get home and clean up.

A voice whispered close to her ear. She whirled around, instant hate flooding through her veins. How dare he get so close!

"Don't be so skittish, my dear. Have a nice dinner?"

"I don't know you. What business is it of yours?"

"I'm always interested in the progress of fellow travelers."

She saw him now in the gloom. Tall, dark, handsome, dressed in black, the usual combo. Valeska found most of the male members of her kind rather tedious. The males took the business of feeding far too seriously, as if it was some kind of high art form, or philosophical lifestyle. To Valeska it was just food and sex. No need to make such a fuss about it.

"I know you," the stranger said.

"Do you now?" said Valeska. "I don't know you, so fuck off."

"So much irritation at such a late hour. You should be happy. You have a full belly."

Valeska was instantly wary. Normally her kind kept to themselves. Only monthly meetings to keep track of everyone's movements, so there would be no accidental impingements on hunting territories. What did this one want?

"Tell me, are you Sanguine or Seminal?" he asked.

"None of your business."

"You're obviously out of touch. Haven't you heard the news?"

"What news?" Valeska asked.

"War," the stranger replied.

"Oh shit."

"Exactly. Yakov the Supplanter has declared war on all Seminals. He managed to convince the High Council that Seminals are . . ."

". . . the whores and hookers of our kind, I know." Valeska's new acquaintance couldn't immediately tell whether she was Seminal or Sanguine and she was giving nothing away.

"What's in it for him?" Valeska asked. "Don't we have enough problems in this fucking world without going to war with each other?"

"Exactly my thoughts," he said. "I figure it's some kind of power play. The Seminals always were contemptuous of his leadership and this is his revenge now that he's got a whiff of power."

"This is bad." Valeska kept her eyes on the male, but she still felt anxious. She could take him, she knew she could. One secret that the Seminals kept to themselves was the knowledge that they were physically stronger than the Sanguines. Maybe that's why Yakov had declared war. Although the Sanguines were weaker, there were more of them, simply because both male and females could be Sanguines, but only females could be Seminals.

It was too late when she realized that someone else had moved in behind her. Valeska attempted to turn around, but a crushing blow at the back of her neck sent her to the ground.

It was a bad year for humanity in 1348. Famine, lousy weather, war and high taxes had weakened the population for years, so when the Great Pestilence came, few people could resist its ravages. Millions died and there was death and corruption everywhere. Rulers feared that their lifestyles might decline, so instead of giving their suffering populations a break, they just raised taxes. The doctors and priests who might have helped combat the disease were the first to succumb to it. Spread by the fleas living on rats, the cities were the worst hit, especially since the ignorant blamed witchcraft for the Plague and set about eradicating one of the few creatures that might have helped the situation: cats, whose reputation for being familiars of the Devil made them more repellant to the God-fearing than the rats who were actually causing the problem. Good hygiene was unknown, medicine was just magical thinking, the concept of germs centuries in the future. There was no cure and no way of knowing how the disease was spreading—so humanity didn't stand a chance. Worldwide, 75 million people were wiped off the planet, over 25 million in Europe alone.

Of course, there were too many people in the world anyway, so it wasn't such a great loss. More food for the rest, if you were in the fortunate percentile that survived. If one possessed lucky gene CCR5 Delta 32, then you were laughing. Not only would you not catch the disease, your descendants would be immune from future horrors like HIV, smallpox and other plagues.

The best place to hide out from the effects of the disaster was to live in one of the hidden mountain villages in Eastern Europe. Strangers had always been treated with suspicion in these places, now more than ever. It was common to kill those wanderers who were Jews, or Gypsies, or lepers, or even those with an unfortunate skin disease like acne. These travelers were never particularly liked in the first place, but now the mistrustful villagers could execute them for a good reason.

It was into this world that a new subspecies of human was born; one created out of necessity and famine; raised up by a ruthlessness of purpose—the primary source of which was to survive—survive at all costs. It began in a small village called Nitra in Moravia. Although spared the brunt of the Plague, it still suffered from the consequences of a remorseless shortage of food. What little was left of supplies was rotted by the incessant rainfall. Ergot fungus infected the main staple of rye bread and many townspeople suffered from the resultant hallucinations and the painful burning sensations of the skin brought on by Ergotine poisoning. One survivor compared it to being burnt at the stake. The people were in despair and there was no one to help or advise them.

One night, a woman called Tasya Renenyko was trying to feed her infant. Her breasts were shrunken and starvation had dried up her mother's milk. Her child cried feebly and Tasya was desperate. She took a knife, carefully sliced across one of her veins and dripped her blood into the child's mouth, open in greedy readiness like a baby bird. The infant suckled her wrist and then stopped after a while, seemingly satisfied.

When her husband Petyr came home, Tasya told him how she had fed their child. He was horrified. He quoted Deuteronomy 12:23 at her: "Only be sure that thou eat not the blood: for the blood is the life; and thou mayest not eat the life with the flesh." Petyr threatened to go to the local priest and report her as a witch who was trying to turn their child into a vampire.

Tasya said, "Which is better: a starving child, or a child that drinks blood? What does it matter, as long as our child lives?"

Petyr retorted, "It matters if the child loses his immortal soul! Better he should die than that happen."

Tasya looked at him and realized that he had become insane with hunger. As far as she was concerned, God (if he existed at all, which she was beginning to doubt) took care of those who took care of themselves. Petyr was heading towards the door to inform on her when Tasya made a snap decision that was to save her life and the life of her child. She grabbed a heavy cast iron pot and with all of her strength, brought it down on the back of Petyr's head; stubborn, stupid, fanatical bastard that he was.

Tasya made sure that he was dead and then went to work. By the end of the day, she had prepared his flesh; preserving, cooking and salting enough of it so that Tasya and her child could survive. She drained his body of blood first; putting the liquid in every available jar she could find and then stored the jars in the cool, dark cellar. She later mixed Petyr's coagulated blood with spices and buckwheat to cook up a delicious, kishka-like sausage. She boiled his bones and scrapped off the last remaining bits of meat. She even cracked open his bones and extracted the precious protein-rich marrow. Tasya then waited until dark, wrapped up the bones in an old blanket, and buried them in the forest.

Petyr was gone, but in a way, he lived on in the most useful way possible, as food for the baby and herself. It was finally quiet around the house and she felt as if a huge weight had been lifted from her heart.

Few people asked about Petyr's whereabouts. He wasn't a popular man and if anyone did query his disappearance, she just said that he had run away, deserting his loved ones for fresher pastures.

Tasya shared some of the precious liquid and flesh with her family and friends and they were terribly grateful. She mixed the blood into soups, so no one could detect the real origins of the protein that was making them feel stronger. Even with Petyr's store of fleshy protein available, she would still open a vein every night and give the baby a sip of fresh blood.

Slowly and surely, Tasya brought those closest to her into her confidence. She explained to them that it was a matter of survival. What was the good of following the Bible and going to Church if you died of hunger or disease? The Lord had deserted humankind, that much seemed evident and they were all on their own now.

It was a secret that they all shared. And it was agreed that when one of their number died, they would divide up his or her body and make the best use of it.

There was some talk in the village. Why was this particular group of people doing so well, when everyone else was suffering so badly? Tasya was well aware of the rumors. She called together her group of thirty or so individuals and told them that the best thing they could do was move some place even more remote and uninhabited, where they could go about their business without comment.

And so the group of blood drinkers quietly packed up their belongings one night and left Nitra, heading east, deeper into the mountains and dark forests, far away from the prying eyes of the clergy and the suspicious townspeople, as well as the ever-present dangers of the Plague. They made a pact where they all agreed that they were the most important people in the world. All others were expendable. They were allowed to do anything to survive. They were the chosen ones—the Sanguine—

following a difficult path of blood worship—perhaps taking Christ's words a bit too literally—enjoying the blood and flesh of their personal saviors in the guise of passersby, travelers and merchants that they met on the road.

Following the lead of Tasya, they lost their faith in a higher power and relied only on each other. They examined each newborn child carefully, noting worrying defects, and killing and feeding on the infant if it was weak and prone to illness. They didn't feel that this was cruel, as a matter of fact; they felt they were doing the child a favor. In such a pitiless world, there was no point living if one was weak and helpless. Each child of the Sanguine was raised to be self-reliant and to use their ingenuity.

Members of the order were sent to the cities for a few years in the guise of priests to acquire knowledge and bring back books so the growing populace could be educated. The common practice of the time was to regard all knowledge that wasn't in the Bible as dangerous. The Sanguine believed the opposite. They felt that they had to explore and find out as much as they could. Living in ignorance was too dangerous.

Eventually—as the Plague years faded into history, the weather improved and the famine receded—the Sanguine wound down the process of cannibalizing their victims (not such an uncommon practice during this troubled time), but they could not cease the taking of the blood. Their bodies had become too dependent on it and they saw no reason to stop.

The next step in the evolution of the Sanguines came in a way that they could not have anticipated. They were aware of the myths of vampires and laughed at them. They didn't believe in the undead, or crosses, or fangs. They were thoroughly grounded in the here and now, in reality, in scientific inevitability, not legends. They knew that to survive, they had to be strong and ruthless, and so they were. But they took precautions to make sure that they were never noticed or picked out as unusual or unique, because that would mean discovery and most certainly, death. They hid their books and writings, they pretended to do menial jobs, and they kept underground and on the fringes of society as much as they could.

The event that changed things was a rape of a young Sanguine girl called Patrizia one day in 1692. The girl refused to say what her attacker looked like or what the circumstances were of the crime against her, which was unusual, as most Sanguines were of a vengeful nature when it came to their own kind. The Elders of her group were concerned when she fell pregnant, because they didn't want a stranger to dilute the precious Sanguine bloodline, but Patrizia refused to abort the fetus. When the child was born, the Elders examined it closely and saw to their alarm and admiration, that the baby was exceptional: healthy, strong, almost unnaturally powerful and aware. The child was so unique that the Elders insisted that Patrizia tell them about the father.

Patrizia was walking by herself one warm autumn's day, through a field of ripe wheat near her home. She felt no anxiety. Most girls her age wouldn't think of going out unaccompanied in the remote area where her people lived, but she was a Sanguine, strong and fearless, so it didn't even enter her mind that she was doing something foolish. Virgin though she was, she had been trained to see off any normal human man and she had nothing to fear from her own kind.

She continued her walk, her mind occupied by her studies, when she stopped, abruptly aware that she was no longer alone. The birds were no longer singing, insects were quiet and the wind had died down. In the far distance, she could hear the shouts of some Sanguine children playing and there was a capricious breeze playing with the treetops in the nearby forest, but here, in the field, all had stopped dead.

She glanced to her right and that's when she saw a man standing at the edge of the woods. He was dressed in black and wore a large wide-brimmed hat that shadowed his face, but she knew that he was looking at her and this terrified her. Now Patrizia was not a fanciful girl: she didn't believe in monsters and demons, and she was not easily frightened, but she knew that she was facing something unknown here. Although it wasn't that hot, it was as if she was looking at the man through a heat haze. The air couldn't hold still around him.

Fear trickled down her groin to her thighs like ice water and her legs felt weak. She had to get out of here, every instinct told her to run, but she knew that if she took her eyes off him for a second, he would be at her side. Of course, this was impossible; he was far away from her. She had a good head start, but although her mind screamed at her to run, she could not instruct her legs to action.

The distant figure in black moved slightly and raised his hand, as if to wave at her. It took every effort on Patrizia's part not to urinate with panic. She turned away from the man and tried to run, but her legs would not cooperate and she fell to the ground, helpless. Up until that moment, Patrizia did not believe in magic or witchcraft, but she knew that something was toying with her, playing with her as if she was a doll and there was nothing she could do about it.

Determined to meet her fate face to face, she turned over so she could see her attacker. She lay on her back and looked up at the blue sky and the white clouds. She shut her eyes for a second and then she knew he was there with her. The fear filled her with ice again and she had to force her eyes open.

He was standing above her. Just looking. Patrizia's heart almost stopped. She knew he was not an ordinary man, but he wasn't Sanguine either. He was handsome in a cruel, wolf-like way. He smiled hungrily and that's when she saw that his canine teeth were filed into sharp points.

He knelt down beside her. He said, "My name is Varazlo. I've been watching you. You are different. Quite exceptional. That's why you are still alive."

Patrizia tried to speak, but he gently put two fingers on her lips. Then he lay down beside her and slowly unbuttoned her dress, exposing her young, tender breasts to the light. She nearly passed out as he bent over her and began to tenderly suck her nipples. Patrizia was shocked at her body's violent reaction to his touches. It was almost agonizingly pleasurable. She felt that her body was a traitor: she was terrified, but her body was aroused beyond measure.

Patrizia's legs shuddered and opened wide of their own accord. He placed his hand between her legs. There was no pretense of surrender on her part. Patrizia knew she was lost and she didn't care. Her hands became her own again and she grabbed her skirts and hoicked them above her waist. Varazlo chuckled with delight at her enthusiasm. He casually ripped off her underwear and placed his cold fingers inside her. These were sensations that she had never experienced before. And she was sure that there was something otherworldly about them.

Varazlo whispered, "You're untouched. You are perfect for me. Tell me you want me. Say it now." She obeyed him, "I want you. Take me. Do what thou wilt." He smiled that wolf-like grin and licked his lips. The movements of his fingers became more urgent. Patrizia's head fell back, her mouth open. He leaned over and kissed her. Her groin bounced up and down frantically and then she came for the first time in her young life. The wave of water flowed through her again, but this time it was deliciously scalding hot. Her legs pummeled the ground and she thought she was going to die. How long could these sensations last?

Varazlo stood up and pulled off his clothes, looking around him to make sure they were still alone. His body was thin, pale-skinned and muscular. He stood between her legs and looked down at her again. Patrizia now knew how the rabbit felt before the wolf pounced. She saw the stranger's manhood standing at attention and spread her arms and her legs out as wide as they could go in total surrender. She looked up at the sky and the clouds again. She didn't know how this was going to end, but she was past caring. He had done something to her. Her passivity amazed her, but she wanted him inside her now, she knew that. And he knew it too.

Varazlo lay down on top of her and he gently pushed himself inside. It hurt, but the pain was different somehow. She wrapped her legs around his waist. He began to move rhythmically inside her. His face hovered over hers, smiling his big hungry wolf smile. Then he dove down on her breast again and this time he bit her with those sharpened teeth of his. Oh, the beautiful agony. His groin movements became more urgent while he sucked her blood.

It was then that Patrizia realized what this creature was. He was Sanguine, but not any kind of Sanguine she knew of. He had some kind of infernal power over her.

His head came up, his mouth smeared with her blood and she tried to scream but she was too weak. All was pain and pleasure inside her.

She tried to tell him to stop, tried to tell him that she was a blood drinker too, but it was impossible, this event was too immense for her mind to take in. Varazlo dove down on her neck and bit her again. She cried out and tried to push him away, but it was hopeless. He was taking her blood and for a moment, she saw the irony of being killed in the same manner as so many of her people's victims. But to go in this way, while he was taking her virginity along with her life, was almost too poignant.

She came again and her cries alerted him. He stopped and concentrated on his own pleasure. He came spectacularly—his face contorted and almost terrifying in its ferocity. His orgasm lasted a long time and with every thrust, she seemed to lose more energy.

Finally, Varazlo stopped. She lay there, breathing shallowly, barely conscious, thinking that this was it; he was going to kill her now. He reached over to a leather satchel and pulled out a knife. The thought of being stabbed to death terrified Patrizia, but there was nothing she could do to stop this powerful, crazed being. If he wanted her life, he could have it.

Varazlo turned to her and showed her the knife. It was beautiful: shiny, engraved with strange runic signs, long and thin. It was a fine blade to end a young girl's life with. He smiled again, leaned over her face and then slowly, sensually cut his wrist for her. Blood seeped out of the wound. He had cut across the vein rather than along it, so the blood wasn't coming out too quickly. He tenderly placed his wrist to her mouth and she greedily drank from him. When the blood coagulated, he made another cut and she fed again. Then he bit her other breast and drank from her. Then he gave his penis to her, stained with her own blood and she sucked it clean, arousing him to orgasm. She drank his seminal fluid and found a new kind of energy flowing through her veins.

They fed on each other until he called a stop. He lay next to her as before, on his side, caressing her body. Varazlo placed an elegant pale hand on her belly.

"I've given you a child today. A girl. All things begin with the female."

In spite of her ordeal, Patrizia laughed. "How could you know?"

Varazlo looked at her intently, "That's what I do. I travel the world and spread my seed."

Hours later, Patrizia staggered back to her village. She kept her secret until she was forced to reveal what happened to her. And now the Elders had to decide what to do with her child, Valhavia, who was obviously the spawn of some kind of super Sanguine no one had ever heard of. Patrizia was adamant. She would leave her people and take her child with her, if the decision was death. But the Elders were intrigued and decided to let the child live. Perhaps this was a sign, a new direction for their people. An injection of a different kind of gene pool, one that would strengthen them and give them more purpose.

Valhavia, her children and their descendants eventually evolved to become a new kind of vampire, one that sucked energy and potency from human males only. The Seminals thrived throughout the centuries, although there were the occasional skirmishes with their cousins. They kept their distance from Sanguines except to mate—a violent ritual that both parties enjoyed, even though surviving the experience could be tricky. All male children were immediately handed over to be brought up by the Sanguines, while all females were kept and raised exclusively by Seminals. Although Seminals were superior in every way, the Sanquines looked down on them for reasons that were just as illogical as most of the human motivations for racism and misogyny.

Valeska was lying in the center of a spotlight at the bottom of a shadowy abyss. She roused herself and slowly crawled to a pathway at the edge, pulling herself up the sides of the cliff to the surface, where she could see a faint glimpse of light.

Then there was a sound: the roar of a thousand voices in her ears. All those souls that she had consumed over the years. They were coming for her. The noise manifested itself as flocks of vicious white ravens, which flew up from the abyss and attacked her, pecking her. Trying to grab her and drag her back down to oblivion. She fought hard against the ravens, trying to ignore the sighs of disappointment: the regret of being ripped out of existence before their time. Valeska had sucked the essence out so many humans and now they wanted justice. Not to mention the millions of pre-humans-as-semen that had been ingested by her voracious appetite. But her will was stronger and she forced her way out of the flocks of screaming ghostly ravens and climbed to the surface. She broke through the barrier of unconsciousness and awoke with an unaccustomed grogginess and an aching head. Her eyes opened slowly, while her brain tried to figure out what had gone wrong with her evening, which had started out so promisingly.

Valeska was lying on top of a large, luxuriant bed, in a dimly lit, extravagantly furnished room. Something bad had happened to her, she knew it. There was a feeling of violation and an unmistakable signs of a quickening of life in her womb. She had been raped while she'd been unconscious, which was an unpardonable contravention of the rules and regulations of her kind. No matter how foul the disagreements had been over the years, rape was unheard of between Sanguines and Seminals.

She got up slowly and cautiously—first going over to the door to check it out, discovering that it was powerfully built and securely locked. Then Valeska walked over to the window, drew back the heavy velvet curtains and discovered that the window had been bricked in.

She heard a chuckle and whirled around to see the door had been opened and a man dressed from head to toe in black was standing in the doorway staring at her. Her anger instantly flared, then flatlined into cold dread. As far as she could tell, he was no human, but he gave no indication that he was one of her kind either. He seemed vaguely familiar to her and she realized with a start that he looked like the legendary Varazlo, the stranger who had impregnated Patrizia, the mother of the Seminals. He had been immortalized in countless portraits by the more artistic of their kind.

The man in black chuckled again: "I see that you recognize me. Very perceptive of you."

Valeska was frozen to the spot. She tried to speak, but was unable to. Varazlo was exerting some kind of paralyzing power over her. The sense that he was the one responsible for her violation was overwhelming.

"To answer the question in your eyes, yes, I took you while you slept. You are perfect for me," he said.

Valeska's rage returned. No man took her without her permission, even the supposed father of her kind. With enormous effort, she whispered, "How dare you. You know our laws."

Varazlo threw his head back and laughed. "Laws are not made for the likes of me, my dear. Your ancestor Patrizia found out the same thing on that warm autumn's afternoon all those centuries ago. I sought you out as I did her. Unfortunately, my time here is limited, otherwise I would have waited until you had awakened, so you could have enjoyed yourself as much as I did."

"Your arrogance is astonishing," Valeska replied.

"Yes, but so well-deserved. I am arrogant because I am the Father of the Seminals. These ridiculous spats between Seminals and Sanguines bore me, so it is time to create a new race of vampires that will destroy the ones that came before it. Your child will be the first of this new race. You must protect him before he comes into the era of his power."

"How am I supposed to protect him if there is another war?"

"Oh, that was just a ruse to distract you while my men brought you to me. There is no war. Not now. But there will be soon, so you must prepare yourself."

"How on earth will I do that?"

"I will give you the means. You will be taken to a place of safety in the Old World, near Nitra, where the Sanguines originated. There is a castle there, riches, slaves and henchmen who will protect you and help you raise our son."

"The stories say that everything begins with the female. Why a son this time?"

"It had to be this way. This will change everything."

Varazlo turned to shut the door and the spell was briefly broken. Valeska realized that this would be her only break for freedom; to shatter the sentence he had placed on her. Not for Valeska imprisonment in some faraway castle, like a demented fairy tale. "Your fate is what you make . . ." and she took her chance.

Valeska launched herself through the air, colliding with Varazlo and knocking him against the fortified door. He slumped to the ground, half-unconscious. She dragged him by his feet into the room, checked the empty corridor, and then shut the door. Going through his pockets, she found the key to the room amongst other talismans and ancient runic amulets, along with a long, silver, thin-bladed knife, a set of hefty old keys, and a wallet full of cash and stolen credit cards.

Valeska undid his belt, pulling his pants down, exposing his penis. Varazlo was still groggy and tried to push her away, but she jumped up, grabbed a silver candlestick from a nearby table and brutally hit him on side of the head. Blood seeped from his mouth and he stopped moving. Valeska listened for his heartbeat. It was still going strong.

She took Varazlo's penis into her mouth and sucked with all her Seminal strength. He stirred. Even unconscious, he must have sensed that things were not going to plan. Valeska, the strongest of her kind, the angriest of her kind, tongued and sucked and drank up Varazlo's very essence and power. His penis stiffened in spite of himself and he groaned. She mounted him—on top and in control. Her Seminal vagina took over and just as he was awakening, Varazlo came and Valeska took enormous joy from slowly draining him of his life.

Varazlo howled and his limbs thrummed and vibrated as if he was being electrocuted—experiencing the extremes of ecstasy as he expired.

Valeska looked into Varazlo's icy blue eyes and he whispered: "You fool. You've killed us both. You cannot protect our child alone."

Valeska leaned over and panted into his ear: "What child? He will not survive this night."

Varazlo spat out: "Bitch!", but she saw the fear in his eyes and she laughed with her first orgasm as he died during his last—gurgling curses at her. She rode him into death and the final darkness of the void. She continued to enjoy herself, feeling more alive and stronger than she'd ever experienced, knowing that by taking Varazlo's life, she had made herself just as powerful as he was.

She cleaned up and gathered up everything that had belonged to him. She stripped him of his clothes and put them on. She emptied her purse and put everything into a black leather satchel that she'd found in the closet. She took all of her clothes and burned them in the fireplace. She unceremoniously shoved Varazlo's body under the bed with his shoes, the only things that she couldn't adapt to wear herself. She was barefoot, but she didn't care.

When Valeska was ready to leave, she listened at the door and was momentarily alarmed to hear the sound of voices nearby. Then she remembered what she was now: not just a woman, not just a Seminal, but something else. There was a knock at the door and she opened it to find the man who had accosted her on the street earlier in the evening, accompanied by another who must have been the one who had attacked her.

They gawked at her—dressed in their leader's clothes—and she gazed without emotion at them. There was a pause and then Valeska audaciously went on the attack, snatching up the silver candlestick and bashing the first man over the head so hard that he dropped pole-axed to the floor. His companion grabbed her and they struggled desperately in the corridor, until she pushed him violently into the wall and felled him with a vicious well-aimed kick straight to his genitals. Valeska reached into the leather satchel and grabbed Varazlo's silver blade. She briskly cut the men's throats—arterial spray spurting across the cream-colored wall. Valeska didn't waste any time and quickly exited the building—finding herself somewhere in the rundown harbor district of the old part of town.

Valeska walked by the docks in the early morning drizzle. She didn't feel the cold. She didn't feel the rain. She didn't bother going home. Her enemies knew where she lived now. She had to start all over again in a different town, a different country, perhaps even a different continent, but first she had a big decision to make about the creature growing in her womb. Not just for her, but for the future of her kind . . .

THE CILICIUM PANDORIC

(Part II of the Cilicium Trilogy)

"Hell Needs a Little Glamour . . ."

Sister Cilice was a first level Female Cenobite of the Order of the Gash and she was bored . . . She yearned for a break from the eternity of exquisite, controlled experimentation on those souls whose reckless pursuit of pleasure for its own sake had led them to the Cenobites. She paced her ascetic, lead-lined, monkish cell in the Second Quadrant of the Labyrinth, ignoring the squawking pleas of her pet crow Xibalbá, who constantly begged for his favorite treat of human eyeballs marinated in red wine.

She fancied a little weekend jaunt away from Hell's environs, so Sister Cilice resolved to visit the Toymaker, a legendary creator of Pandorics, unique playthings and mechanical birds. And she'd never been to Paris, a fabled city that was considered far too sinful when she was enduring her first incarnation as a desolate, sex-starved nun in a dismal, run-down convent in the Vendée region of Western France.

Sister Cilice was fascinated by the idea that a mere human could somehow construct the glittering, mysterious Pandoric boxes that could invoke her hellish cohorts so readily. This was especially intriguing to her, because her method of conjuring up the Schism and becoming one with the Order of the Gash had been so different from the others of her ilk. Sister Cilice's ceremony had involved offerings of blood and roses, a discreet sacrifice of a sick child, and chanting the incantations of the corrupt monk and sorcerer, Raphael Athanasius. (Athanasius had been a *compadre* to the infamously depraved 15th century French general, child serial killer and spendthrift, Gilles de Rais.) Of course, the crowning ingredient in her infernal recipe was . . . desire.

Sister Cilice slipped into the Lead Cenobite's quarters and "borrowed" the Ianua Mechanism, a device of luminous beauty whose platinum and obsidian components were fashioned from the designs of 14th century alchemist extraordinaire, Albertus Magnus, which he in turn had borrowed from the Greek mathematical and engineering genius, Archimedes. It was the only device that could open the rarely used Reverse Schism to enable the Cenobites to freely travel to the dimension of *Homo sapiens*—without the participation of humans themselves. Under the strict rules that governed the use of the Ianua Mechanism, Sister Cilice wasn't allowed to use it for her own purposes, but as it was employed so infrequently, she doubted that the Lead Cenobite would notice it was missing.

Sister Cilice travelled through the time portal—arriving at the Toymaker's eccentric residence in the artisans' quarter of 18th century Paris in an instant. Rematerializing in a corridor outside his workshop located in the basement *cave* underneath his house, Sister Cilice entered the arched doorway to find him kneeling on the stone floor, deeply involved in the process of strangling yet another prostitute. (Prostitutes were easy prey for the Toymaker. He was able to entice them to his house for the price of a loaf of bread, where he killed them and boiled them down to their base components. The fatty deposits under their stomach muscles were an essential constituent for the greasing of the Pandoric's precious gears.)

Sister Cilice intuitively knew that the naked young prostitute's last moments were nigh, as her body was going through some thrillingly spasmodic death throes, so she stopped time for a moment. The Toymaker was frozen, but the girl was in Sister Cilice's cocoon of time and space. She swooped down and clamped her lips over the girl's wide open, imploring mouth. Sister Cilice was delighted by the girl's warm, velvety tongue squirming inside her mouth. She sucked in the girl's last breath—vacuuming up her soul in the bargain. The young prostitute juddered, thrashed her voluptuous, pale thighs against the floor and died.

Sister Cilice stepped back behind the Toymaker and resumed time. She was amused to see him trying to kiss the dead prostitute—no doubt hoping to get a taste of her last honeyed breath himself. When he realized that the wretched whore had already expired, he released his grasp around her neck with such disappointed abandon that her head dropped to the floor with a thud. This caused Sister Cilice to rasp out a desiccated laugh. The Toymaker swung around in surprise and anger, then fell prostrate on the floor with respect and humility, not expecting to see such a distinguished visitor without prior notice. He dared to raise his eyes to drink in her deathly presence: the dead blue-white skin; the bloodstained, black, tight-fitting, leather nun's habit; the silver piercings that lashed through her face; the open wounds that would never heal; and the baleful, emerald-green eyes that looked at him with such scorn.

"Get up, Toymaker, and show me these wonders of yours," Sister Cilice demanded. He leapt to his feet and proudly presented his wares: intricate, beautiful, artistic, musical Pandorics that would have astonished her if she was still human. However, even Sister Cilice could admire his handiwork, especially knowing the malevolent secrets and terrors of visceral carnality that the boxes could unleash upon their chosen supplicants.

Then an idea popped into her rebellious mind. It had always annoyed Sister Cilice that she was a *Subordinatus* to the Lead Cenobite. She wanted her own order, her own "scream" of demons. In her midnight plottings, she had already given the New Order a name: "The Sisterhood of the Cilice." The idea of adding more females under her command to populate the vast dungeons of the Underworld was a delicious one. After all, Hell needed a bit of glamour.

"Toymaker, I want you to make a special Pandoric dedicated to me and me alone. A Cilicium Pandoric that will attract needy females desiring the ultimate in sensuality—with designs incorporating things of special meaning to me: blood-red roses, a murder of my favorite, vermillion-eyed crows (and how I delight in that particular collective noun) and silver cilices."

The Toymaker was a bit hazy on what a cilice exactly was, so she showed him, lifting her long leather skirt to reveal her legs and vulva entwined with silver chains. The chains were adorned with tiny hooks that stabbed into her bloodstained flesh—the *sanguineus* fluids long dried and blackened. Like the hair shirts of old, cilices were designed to remind the wearer of the suffering of the Savior. Ironic that they had become part and parcel of Sister Cilice's depraved sexual fantasies back in her old life at the convent, before her Rapture—before her transformation into the dark-hearted demonic angel that she now was.

As they discussed the designs, Sister Cilice came up with her *pièce de résistance:* the alchemical symbol for female, ♀—which was also a representation of the Greek goddess of love, Venus—had to be stamped on each box.

For two weeks, the Toymaker obediently labored over the design and construction of the Cilicium Pandoric, while a veiled Sister Cilice explored and enjoyed the seamier elements of Paris during the dead of night.

As instructed, the Toymaker was to test the box before delivery, so he plotted to meet with the beautiful, but notorious Duchess de Mortamour, whose reputation for everything transgressional was chattered about under the breaths of the powerful men and women of the court, but never out in the open. The duchess's husband, the Duke de Mortamour, was far too influential with the king and no one dared to cross him.

The duchess was an admirer of the so-called Blood Queen, the Hungarian Countess Elizabeth Báthory de Ecsed, who was reputed to have killed over 600 women and young girls in the early 17th century so she could bathe in their blood in order to maintain her youthful appearance. The duchess was also reputed to have dabbled in the dark arts and murdered a few young women herself, but since many of these rumors centered on women that the duke himself had dallied with, her bloodthirsty streak may have had more to do with jealousy than magic.

The Toymaker made an appointment with the duchess, promising her an intriguing Pandoric with bold motifs laced with intricate textures. His reputation preceded him and the duchess was eager to inspect his workshop.

A time was set for her appointment just after midnight. As instructed, she hadn't told anyone of the assignation and arrived veiled and dressed in black via a hired coach and four.

The Toymaker escorted her to his workshop and the duchess was suitably impressed with not only the array of Pandorics laid before her, but also the lifelike mechanical birds that tweeted melodiously in the background. He took the duchess to a small private room in the back, where the Cilicium Pandoric was displayed on a table dressed as an altar next to some dried red roses and a decanter full of unspecified red liquid.

"Behold, my masterpiece, designed for your pleasure!" the Toymaker proclaimed with a wave of his hand. The duchess moved forward to examine the box and he withdrew from the room discreetly. He entered a nearby closet and removed a small portrait from the wall. Secreted behind the portrait was a peephole, where he could spy on the proceedings in the private room.

The duchess picked up the pandoric, admiring its silver, ebony and ruby encrusted designs. Her hands flew over the surface—moving the beautifully engineered segments as if she had designed it herself, then she stopped suddenly and put down the pandoric, as she was overcome with an almost stultifying wave of heat and nausea. Sweat broke out on her brow and her silken clothes, so comfortable before, became scratchy and burdensome—almost burning her skin. She tore at the buttons at her throat, trying to remember how the dress came off, because she was so used to maids dressing and undressing her.

In desperation, the duchess resorted to frantically rending the dress from her body, finally collapsing in a naked heap on the floor. It was then that she heard the discordant but compelling, tinkling melody of the Pandoric calling to her. She dragged herself up the altar, exhausted and burning with an internal fire. She swept the roses and decanter off the altar and lay down on her back—the Pandoric in her hands, fingers fiddling with the moving panels, feverishly desiring an answer, craving an escape from her boring life at court, yearning for a sensuality beyond anything offered here on earth. The device felt her wet, pulsating fingers and heard her panting desires and the panels began to move by their own accord, fashioning themselves into a different kind of mechanism—one designed to give pleasure to solitary women.

The duchess was thrilled at this new love toy and placed the Pandoric between her legs. She slowly inserted it inside her vagina, which was more than ready to embrace the device's vibrating pleasures. At first, the experience was almost overwhelming—more than any man had given her over her years of debauchery. The duchess shuddered and orgasmed, screaming her release.

Then the noises from the Pandoric changed tune. Its vibrations became more urgent and the duchess became frightened. She tried to pull it out, but felt excruciating pain as tiny hooks sprang from the device and fastened themselves to her vaginal wall. She let go and the pain ceased, but the vibrations became more violent and she came again, fearfully, helplessly. For hours it seemed, she suffered the most exquisite, carnal sensations until she was nearly foaming at the mouth.

Finally, the Pandoric stopped its infernal pulsations. She cautiously pulled it out, gazing with wonder and exhaustion at the bloodstained device. That's when she realized that she was no longer alone.

Sister Cilice stood in a dark corner of the room, smiling at her. She had witnessed the whole ritual and she was pleased beyond measure. Here was a woman whose capacity for sensational sexual suffering neared her own. A perfect addition to the Labyrinth.

"Who are you, wretched woman?" the duchess demanded. Sister Cilice smiled her wolfish smile again and said, "You called me, I came. Put the Cilicium Pandoric back where it was and I will show you such pleasures beyond anything you have experienced before."

"I think I've had enough," the duchess declared, attempting to get up, but she was frozen on her back, holding the device above her like a dagger. And then it transformed into something else. And the duchess screamed, but this time it wasn't in pleasure.

Sister Cilice was delighted with the Cilicium Pandoric and rewarded the Toymaker well with five prostitutes that she had found huddling under a bridge during her brief exploration of Paris. She took the damned and mutilated duchess back with her to the Labyrinth, transforming her into an acolyte of the Sisterhood of the Cilice.

The Toymaker went back to murdering prostitutes and creating more Pandorics, never realizing that he may have played an important part in what became known later in hellish circles as The Cicilium Rebellion of the Female Cenobites.

GAIA

J UST HER LUCK TO BE CHRISTENED GAIA, AFTER THE GODDESS personifying the earth. Her mother, determined to fit into American life—and yet still yearning for her old world, Greek roots—thought it was a beautiful name, but this was before the New Age, touchy-feely, environmentalist types popularized the Gaia Theory. Her "weird" name made her withdrawn and unhappy, and bullies made her school life hell.

Gaia's mother would tell her the ancient myths of her homeland, never considering for a moment that these mesmerizing tales of abandoned cruelty could warp a young girl's mind. But they did, especially the one about her namesake, the goddess Gaia, and her abusive husband Uranus, ruler of the starry sky. Created by the goddess as a companion and protector, Uranus soon descended into barbarism and raped her every night. Children popped out of her fertile womb and were promptly stuffed right back in again by Uranus, who was deeply paranoid that any offspring that he created would overthrow him and rule in his stead.

One son that avoided being forced back inside his mother was Cronus. The goddess persuaded him that Uranus was causing her unbearable pain, handed Cronus an enormous flint scythe and told him to sort his father out. Cronus crept into their bed one night, castrated Uranus and threw his blood-soaked genitalia into the sea.

Uranus was deposed, the goddess was finally happy and Cronus ruled until his own son, Zeus, came along to prevail over him. Uranus's genitalia, for some reason known only to the dark minds of antiquated Greeks, metamorphosed into sea foam and then transformed into Aphrodite, the radiant goddess of love.

So, the dark and disturbing myths and legends of early Greece were the backdrop to Gaia's childhood. As her mother cheerfully prattled on about gang rapes, beheadings, familial murders, betrayals and the other brutal goings-on of a time long past, Gaia's imagination conjured up even worse things. Every day, she would walk to school eying the sky with distrust. Would the heavens open and suck her up to Olympus, the mountaintop home of the gods, where they would torture her, dismember her and throw her liver to the vultures? Gaia scuttled to and from school like a depressed beetle, bent over her books, terrified of looking up.

The only time that she felt truly happy was when her Uncle Abraxas was in town. Always travelling—for reasons never specified—Abraxas was not only devilishly handsome, he played a mean bouzouki as well. Evenings graced by his presence were always family affairs: lots of Greek food, dancing and chat. Gaia would put on her favorite red dress and dance for her assembled relatives—folk dances taught to her by her mother. As she whirled past Abraxas, he would admire her white thighs flashing by. He'd smile at her and she felt that maybe the world wasn't so terrible after all.

One night, when Gaia was on the verge of her teenage years, Abraxas hit town again. He seemed haunted and her mother was concerned about him, but Gaia demanded another evening of fun and dancing, and so it was arranged.

That night, Abraxas played his bouzouki like a demon and Gaia danced in an almost ecstatic frenzy. Finally, after a couple of hours, they both had to stop. Although the crowd of relatives demanded more, the performers needed a time out.

Abraxas grabbed Gaia's arm and they went outside to the backyard, sweaty and exhausted. Before she realized what was on his mind, he'd managed to pull her around to the side of the house. Suddenly, he was pushing her up against the wall, sticking his tongue in her mouth—almost sucking the life out of her. She tried to push him off, but he was too strong. He grabbed both of her wrists and held them tightly behind her back with one hand. He stopped kissing her for a moment and stuck the other hand into her mouth. She struggled to say something, but he whispered in her ear: "You are mine, my maenad . . . you tempted me with your dancing and your wantonness. I know you want me. Why are you struggling? This was meant to be."

Gaia stopped moving. The big dark god she'd always feared had finally arrived, not from the sky, but out of a beat-up Chevy Vega. He'd called her a maenad, one of the crazed female followers of the god Bacchus. Abraxas had declared this was meant to be and who was she to question him?

Abraxas breathed ouzo into her face as he took his hand out of her mouth and put it between her legs, ripping her panties off. He entered her and it was a short, nasty, painful experience, but Gaia didn't scream. She just bit her lip and looked up to the skies, praying that, for once, the old gods would come and suck her out of this life and up to Olympus. Unfortunately, the contemporary world continued on in its dirty, squalid way. The sounds of her family enjoying themselves inside her parent's house accompanied her ordeal; their laughing and jokes mixed with Abraxas's grunts of pleasure.

He zipped up his pants and whispered in her ear: "Not a word to your mother, maenad, or worse will befall you. This is between you and me. And she'd never believe you anyway." Abraxas pulled back to look in her eyes. "After all, I am her Golden Boy." He flashed his devilish smile at her and went back into the house.

Gaia stood there for a while, trembling with shock. The pain almost made her faint, but she willed herself to pick up her panties, walk into the house and scurry up the back stairs so no one would see her. She locked herself in the bathroom and ran a bath. She took the ripped panties, wrapped them up tightly in toilet paper and placed them at the bottom of the wastebasket, underneath some other stuff, so no one would find them. She stripped and carefully lowered herself into the bath—lying back and closing her eyes.

The internal pain dissipated gradually. Gaia looked down and saw tendrils of blood coming from between her legs—spreading gently through the water like red ivy. A tear made its way down her face. So, this was the end of her childhood.

She contemplated just slipping under the water and ending it, but then a furious anger rose up inside her. Why should she? She had done nothing wrong. Her uncle was a sick pervert and she wouldn't give him the satisfaction of doing away with herself.

So Gaia, like the earth itself, endured.

Abraxas was arrested a couple of years later in New York State for sex offences regarding a minor. Six months later, he was stabbed in the kidneys with a homemade shiv in the men's showers in Dannemora, dying in agony. Gaia felt great satisfaction, although she had to hide it from her mother, who was devastated: first by the "totally untrue" charges against her little brother, then by his murder.

Gaia kept her head down, went to school, got a degree, never had a date, helped out with her parent's dry cleaning establishment, sat by her mother's bed as she died, sat by her father's bed as he died. After a meeting with her parent's lawyer, she realized that, due to their frugal lifestyles and good business sense, she'd inherited enough money so she never had to work again. In fact, she'd never have to leave the house again, if she didn't want to. And that was her dream.

Gaia hired some builders to construct a room in the basement for her: a totally secure room that no one could enter without her permission. No windows, just air conditioning to keep the room fresh. The walls were painted red, like blood, and she decorated it with luxurious and plush furnishings that made it look like a womb: dark, warm, protected. She had everything she needed, even a kitchenette, bathroom and toilet. No sky god could touch her there. No man could touch her there either.

And yet, if she had to go out, the anxiety, the palpitations, the fear, still accompanied her at every step. Sometimes, when her nerves overcame her, Gaia would stop underneath a tree and peer up through the branches, trying to see if Uranus was coming after her.

The bed in her room was very comfortable, but after a while, she started to feel vulnerable again. She dragged some pillows underneath the bed and slept there.

So Gaia's miserable life spun out its course. She lived in the red room, had her groceries delivered, did everything else online on her computer, exercised religiously in front of the television and felt that she was, if not happy, then at least safe. But someone else had different ideas.

Nat and Genko were typical disaffected youths. They wasted more time and energy trying to commit crimes than being employed in any other useful activity. They'd heard rumors about some rich weird woman who lived at 16 Pandora Crescent, so they plotted a break-in.

The plan was pretty simple: go to the weird lady's house one night, walk around to the back, jimmy open the kitchen door, and rob the joint. They weren't particularly bothered if she was there or not. Both Nat and Genko had fairly unevolved ideas about women. If she woke up and squawked, then they'd rough her up a bit. They'd punched elderly ladies, battered old guys, tortured kids for their mobile phones. A little ultraviolence was never far from their agenda and was, in fact, a big part of the charm of their lifestyle.

One dark, rain-swept, April night, Nat and Genko arrived at Gaia's home, which was cut off from the neighbors by large trees and luxuriant shrubs. Cautiously going around to the backyard, they crept up the steps. They forced the door open with some tools they had stuffed into the waistbands of their tracksuit pants.

Once inside, they produced two Streamlight 88031 flashlights that they'd lifted from a hardware store. Nat and Genko thought they were cool, because the guys on *CSI: Miami* used them. They walked around the kitchen, and then moved into the dining room, pulling out drawers, checking the contents. Their frustration grew as they proceeded into the living room. There didn't seem to be anything of value in this deserted, neglected nuthouse. They went upstairs and checked out the bedrooms: zero, zip, nothing—just the smell of damp and dustsheets everywhere.

They had a quick whispered conference. Their informer, Jerry the delivery guy, brought groceries to the weird lady every week, so where the hell was the bitch?

"Could she be so buggy that she's living in the attic?" Genko asked.

"Hey, man, maybe she's in the basement. Creepy," Nat replied.

"Fuck it, let's split up. You take the basement. I'll check out the attic," Genko ordered.

Genko searched the top floor for access to the attic while Nat clumped down the stairs to the ground floor. By this time, they were both angry that their victim was putting them to so much trouble, and they were past caring whether she'd heard them or not.

Gaia had heard them all right. The house resonated with their footsteps. She was terrified by this invasion of her sanctuary. Had Uranus finally come to pluck her up to the stars, or had he sent his minions to kill her? But then an overwhelming rage rose up inside Gaia. How dare these interlopers break into her home?

She slid out from underneath the bed, rose to her feet, and ran over to her kitchenette. Gaia picked up the biggest and sharpest knife she could find, along with a hefty rolling pin and some additional weaponry. She slipped out of her room into the darkness of the basement, locking the big door behind her.

She could hear noises at the top of the stairs and a naked bulb sputtered into life, casting a weak, watery light throughout the basement. Gaia hid behind the boiler and held her breath. For a moment, she wondered why she'd made this dangerous move. She could have stayed for days in her safe room, daring the intruders to break through the steel-plated door, but her anger pushed her fear away.

Gaia heard someone coming down the stairs. She saw a man walk through the mess that littered the basement, right up to the door of her room.

"Shit, she must have a panic room. Fuck the bitch!" the man muttered to himself. He fumbled around his clothes and produced a crowbar from under his sweatshirt.

He went to work on the door. Gaia tried to decide what to do. He was a young guy, fit and strong. How was she going to overpower him? Then she remembered her mother talking about the genius of Alexander the Great, and how he would use his enemies' stupidity against them. This guy, a poor mortal envelope for the most brutal of gods, certainly seemed stupid enough.

Gaia found a small empty jam jar on a nearby shelf and threw it into the far corner of the basement. The man whipped around in a panic—his attention instantly drawn to the corner. Gaia dashed out into the center of the room, leapt up and smashed the light bulb with her rolling pin, then retreated behind the boiler. The man cursed and scrambled around, feeling for his flashlight.

Gaia, who knew her territory even in the pitch dark, circled around the basement, hugging the walls. The man carefully moved towards the corner, using his flashlight to investigate. She crept up behind him and whacked him on the head with her rolling pin as hard as she could. He fell down to the floor. Gaia picked up his flashlight and illuminated his face. He was out for the count: still breathing, but unconscious.

Gaia found some plastic ties and secured the man's hands behind his back. She paused for a moment, smiled, and decided to send the god of the heavens a little message. Gaia pulled down the intruder's sweat pants. She gingerly retrieved his genitalia and lassoed them with a plastic tie. She pulled the tie as tightly as she could, effectively cutting off the blood supply to the man's penis and testicles. Her prowler would have something to scream about when he woke up.

Genko was still up in the attic, going through some photographs that he'd found in a battered old trunk. The woman who lived here used to be pretty hot when she was young, that's for sure. Then he heard something: a high-pitched, animalistic wailing sound that made the little hairs on the back of his neck stand to attention. Genko realized he'd been wasting precious time looking at stupid useless shit when he was supposed to be searching for treasure. And what the fuck was that racket?

Genko dashed down the stairs to the kitchen. The noise grew louder. It was coming from the basement. He tried the basement light switch, but no luck. He started to rush down the stairs, but stopped halfway, suddenly cautious.

"Where the fuck are you, man? What's going on?" he shouted into the darkness.

"Jesus, Genko, help me! Get your ass down here. Someone's fucked with my Johnson!"

Genko, although alarmed, still didn't budge.

"Are they still around? Who did it?"

Nat screamed, "For fuck's sake, how should I know?"

Genko ran down the stairs, moving with his flashlight through the darkness in the direction of Nat's inconsolable moaning. He found him in a corner, lying amongst some broken glass. Genko was horrified to see Nat's genitals looking hugely purple and swollen, but at least they were attached.

"You're still intact, man. Someone's just cut off the blood supply, that's all. How the fuck did it happen?"

"Just get me loose!"

Instead of kneeling down to help his friend, Genko suddenly turned and swept the light around the basement, surprising Gaia as she crept up behind him, knife at the ready. Genko swung the heavy flashlight and cracked her on the side of the head. Gaia dropped to the floor.

"Well, fuck me. Look at this," Genko said.

Nat, however, was still crying with pain. Genko turned back to his friend and cut the plastic ties, paying special attention to the one looped around Nat's genitalia. The last thing he wanted to do was to accidently castrate his friend.

"Hey, it's okay. Once the blood goes back inside of it, it'll be fine," Genko said, although he was no doctor and Nat's member looked a bit worse for wear.

Nat rolled on the floor, cradling his penis, panting: "Fucking bitch, I'll kill her. Fucking bitch, I'll kill her . . ." over and over again.

Genko glanced over at Gaia, lying helpless on the floor. "We won't kill this one. Yet. She's got some things to tell us. And hey, it's free pussy."

Gaia struggled back into consciousness, but she didn't moan, she didn't open her eyes. She just became aware. She was sitting on a chair, with her arms tied behind her back. So, Uranus had triumphed. His messengers had taken her prisoner and now they would torture her and cut out her liver, but not without dishonoring her first. Her rage rose up again and it took all her resources not to struggle against her bonds.

Nat and Genko observed their prize. They were looking forward to torturing some information out of the bitch.

"Hey, crazy lady, wake up," Genko said, slapping Gaia hard on the cheek.

She opened her eyes and looked up at them. Nat and Genko involuntarily took a step back. Man, this woman was insane. Her witchy eyes burned into them, her hair was everywhere, and blood was trickling from her mouth, staining her teeth red. For one millisecond, Genko thought they should just get the hell out of there, but that was nuts. She was the one tied up, not them. They were in control and she couldn't do a damn thing about it. How cool was that?

Genko leaned into Gaia's face. "So, little lady, tell us where your money is. Where are the keys to that door over there? And while you're at it, give us your pin number for your credit card, or I swear, we'll mess you up so bad that not even your mother will recognize you." Genko hit her again to emphasize his point.

Gaia looked at him dispassionately and spat in his face. Genko was outraged. He moved forward and ripped her nightdress open, exposing Gaia's breasts. Nat whistled in appreciation. Genko grabbed her nipples—twisting them as hard as he could, trying to get a reaction. Gaia bit her lower lip until she drew blood, but she wouldn't give these slaves of Uranus satisfaction.

"Shit, she's a tough little whore," Nat said, as he lit a cigarette. He took a deep drag and then casually placed the lit end on Gaia's shoulder, grinding the cigarette into her flesh. The men were astounded when she didn't scream.

"Man, maybe she's got some kind of nerve disease," Nat observed. Genko was flummoxed. He hit her a couple more times, but the bitch still didn't react. He felt cheated, frustrated and angry by not hearing those delicious female screams.

"Fuck it. Untie her. All this torture shit is making me horny," Genko said.

Nat went around to the back of Gaia's chair and untied her. He grabbed her by the hair and dragged her to the center of the basement, throwing her down on the cold cement floor. He ripped off what was left of her nightdress. She lay there, passively staring at the two men.

"Maybe she's a retard," ventured Nat.

Then Gaia smiled at them. A crazy, sexy smile. She opened her legs wide, exposing herself, and lifted up her arms, mutely beseeching them to come to her. The men looked at each other in astonishment. Wow, this was really out there.

When they turned back to her, Gaia was masturbating, stroking one of her nipples with one hand, pleasuring herself with the other.

Genko got instantly hard. He pulled down his sweatpants and underwear, and lay down on the cement next to her. Nat moved off, as he wasn't really into threesomes. Let Genko have his fun, then he'd have his, then they'd find out where she kept her stuff.

Genko tried to take Gaia's hand away from her pussy, but she was surprisingly strong. She was really going for it: mouth wide open, panting like a dog in heat. Did this wild bitch get off on torture and pain?

Genko was desperate to get inside her hot, wet pussy. He grabbed her hand and pulled it out, not noticing until too late that there was a small sheathed knife in her hand. Gaia pulled off the sheath and stuck the knife into Genko's throat, then ripped it across—disabling his larynx and cutting his carotid artery. Arterial spray fountained out of Genko's neck as he rolled back, trying to stop the flow, but it was too late. The crazy woman was smiling at him again. He was choking on his own blood. He tried to call out to warn Nat, but darkness was coming in fast from all sides.

Nat heard some strange sounds coming from the center of the room, but he ignored them. He was too busy looking at a really nice Black & Decker tool set. He searched the shelves; maybe the crazy lady had hidden her keys there. Then he heard a noise right behind him and he whirled around.

Nat screamed at the sight of a naked, demented, blood-drenched Gaia holding up Genko's severed head by the hair in one hand and a knife in the other. Nat had seen a lot of bad shit go down in his lifetime, but the sight of his friend's decapitated head totally freaked him out. And it wasn't helped by one additional gruesome detail: Genko's penis was stuffed in his mouth. This woman wasn't human and he wasn't going to hang around to see what she had in store for him.

Nat turned and booked for the stairs. Gaia dropped Genko's head and followed at a run. Nat stumbled on the fifth step and Gaia grabbed him by the ankles and brought him down, crawling up his body, stabbing as she went. Nat screamed, trying to get this creature off him, flapping his arms at her like a little old lady. He pissed in his pants as Gaia straddled him on the stairs, stabbing him in the chest over and over. The screaming eventually stopped, but she didn't. Gaia was a killing machine, getting hooked on the rhythm. The rocking of her body, the motion of the stabbing, the rubbing of her genitals on Nat's zipper, all cumulated in a final orgasmic frenzy. She screamed her pleasure as she slashed at Nat's throat, finally cutting through the spinal column and severing his head from his body.

Nat's head rolled off down the stairs and into the darkness of the basement, but Gaia didn't care. She exulted in her victory. She had successfully executed both her intruders; demons sent by the god of the heavens to take her away. She was the powerful one now.

After a while, the ecstasy faded and she disengaged from Nat's headless body. The real world began to intrude. Gaia knew that she needed to clean up the basement and get rid of the bodies, but every muscle ached with the effort of killing the two men.

Gaia went back into her sanctuary, locked the door behind her and had a shower. She dried herself and lay down on the bed, needing a rest before she cleaned up the basement carnage.

She couldn't close her eyes, with all that adrenaline pumping through her body. Gaia looked up at the ceiling and was startled to see a tiny golden light floating in the air like a firefly. The light started to move in concentric circles that slowly spiraled out. She heard a faint whooshing sound with every circle completed, like some distant, celestial helicopter.

Gaia was puzzled more than anything else. She stood on her bed, reaching up with her right hand, trying to touch the ever-increasing, bright spiral of light. She bounced gently on the bed in an attempt to trampoline up to the light. She jumped and her hand entered the spiral and for an instant, Gaia felt a freezing, vacuum-like force pull her hand up, before it lost its grip and dropped her back down.

Gaia landed on the bed and her knees collapsed underneath her. She lay on her back, terrified, and stared at the whirling, galaxy-like, spiral of light. The whooshing noise grew louder, the spiral got bigger and it felt like cold water was being poured over her loins.

Finally after all these years, Uranus, god of the sky, was coming to carry her up to the heavens.

A wave of almost sexual relief flowed through her. If Uranus wanted Gaia, he could have her. She had proved that she was strong enough. She had made blood sacrifice of two of his minions, so that should count for something.

She stood up on her bed again, both arms raised in homage to the swirling golden light. The breeze coming from the vortex lifted her hair up around her face, making her look like a female astronaut serving on board the International Space Station. She bounced one more time and her arms entered the vortex. She felt drawn up, into the blinding, shimmering, yellow light. Something icy cold seized her hands and Gaia was sucked into the arms of her long-lost, lover-rapist god and out of her room in an instant.

The vortex speeded up, reversed, drew into itself, and then disappeared with a distant sizzling crackle.

It didn't take the authorities long to piece together what had happened at 16 Pandora Crescent. Nat and Genko hadn't shown up at their usual watering holes for few days and Jerry, the delivery guy, started to worry when he didn't get any response from the crazy lady, especially since he was the one who'd tipped off the boys in the first place. Jerry called in an anonymous tip and the police checked out the house, discovering the jimmied back door. It was obvious that something bad had happened in the house as soon as they entered the kitchen, judging from the copper-flavored stench coming up from the basement. The officers went down the stairs and found the decapitated bodies of Nat and Genko. One of them threw up on his shoes while the other one called CSU and the big boys.

Homicide and the ME came in to assess the scene. A nasty, brutish end to two nasty brutish lowlifes, is how the lead detective, McPherson, coined it.

But where was the lady of the house? Jerry, the only person who'd ever had any contact with the owner, was escorted into a small, window-less room in the station house and grilled over his part in the mess. He caved easily, bleating that the bad boys had made him spill the beans on the crazy lady and her riches.

McPherson returned to the basement. A couple of heavies called Jace and Bingo were trying to open the door to the panic room, where everyone figured Gaia Iliopoulos must have been living at the time of the break-in, considering the state of the rest of the house.

He wondered what they would find when they finally broke through. Had Ms. Iliopoulos run away from the scene, locking the panic room as she left? Was she still in there, half-starved and scared to death? Had she been wounded in the mêlée and dragged herself into the panic room to die? Had she really killed . . . no, not killed, fucking massacred, those bozos? From what he'd heard, he didn't think it could be possible. She was a shut-in and not known to be a violent individual. But, hey, if you confront a couple of mooks breaking into your house, then maybe you would turn into some kind of avenging Fury.

A shout from Jace broke through McPherson's reverie. They'd managed to cut a hole in the steel plating of the door using oxyacetylene torches. McPherson peered into the room. The lights were on, albeit at a low level, and a computer screen was shining brightly in the corner. "Ms. Iliopoulos? It's the police. Are you okay?" he called. No response. McPherson snaked his arm through the hole, hoping to find a key still in the lock on the inside. He found it, turned it and the door finally opened.

McPherson stood at the entrance, while Jace and Bingo went upstairs for a coffee break. He called out again, but the room looked deserted. He was about to peek under the bed when he decided to check out Ms. Iliopoulos's computer instead. McPherson wandered over to the desk to wiggle the mouse so the screensaver would disappear. He was staring at the computer screen, trying to make sense of the website he was looking at, when an excruciating pain sliced through his spine. For an instant, he thought he'd put his back out, but then he looked down and noticed a large steel blade coming out of his chest. He coughed up blood and collapsed on the floor. He tried to look up as he felt the knife being pulled out of his back; to see what was doing this to him.

A dirty, naked woman was standing over him. He tried to say something as she rolled him over. She started to stab him in the neck, sawing away at his throat. The last thing he saw was her face, lit up by the craziest, sexiest smile.

Guess he should have checked under the bed first after all.

Uranus wanted more blood. Gaia had been sent back from Olympus because another sacrifice was required. That was Gaia's excuse and she stuck to it throughout the trial. Of course, no one believed her, but she didn't care. She was above all this trivial human nonsense of life and death. She was a goddess now and no mortal could take that away from her. Even when she rode the lightning to her final meeting with her god, Gaia had a smile on her face. That crazy, sexy smile.

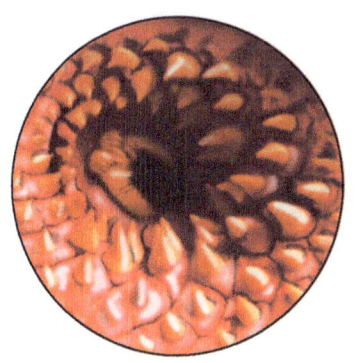

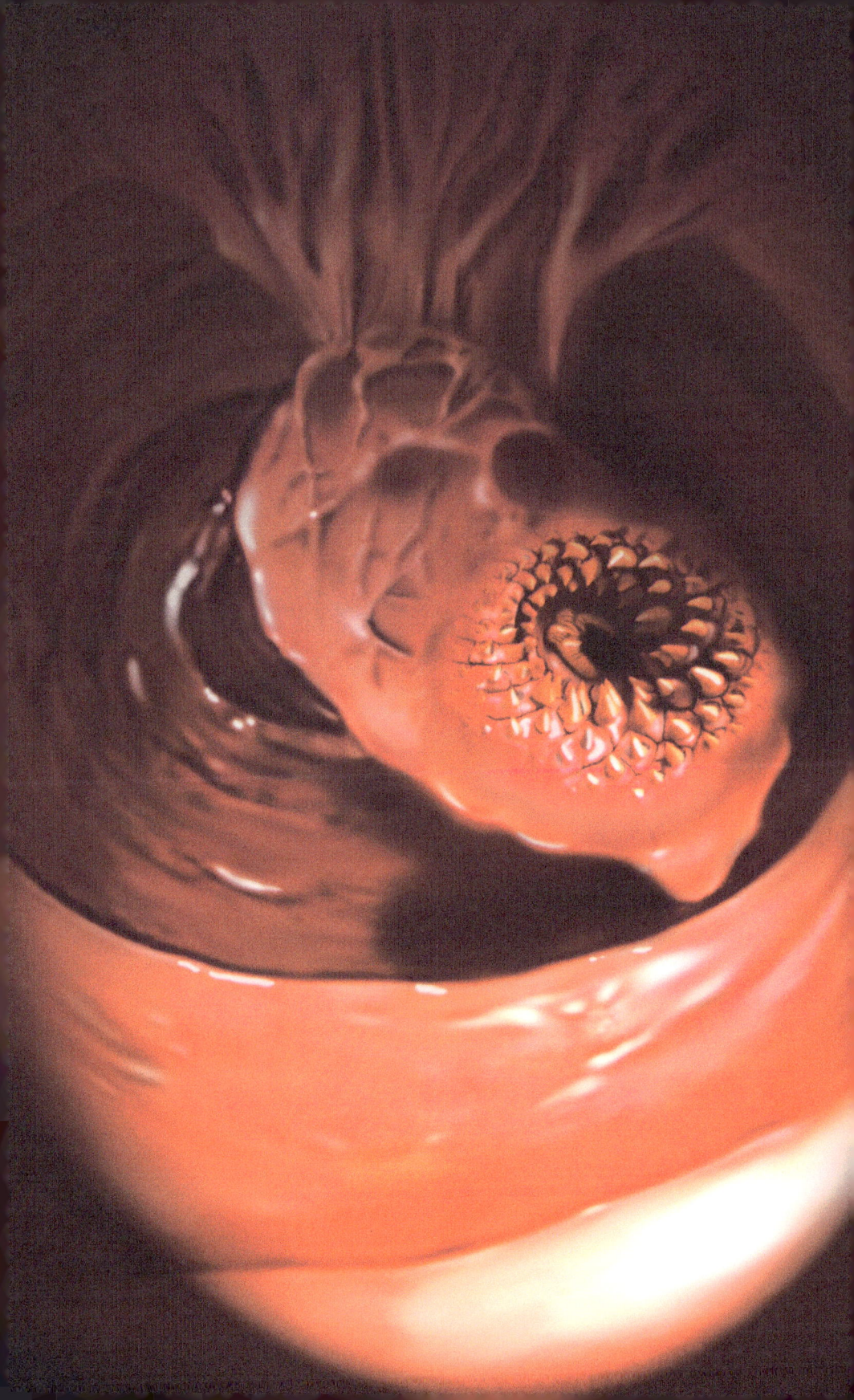

POLYP

"The 'Second Brain' of Your Nightmares"

IN THE DEEP, DARK, SOFTLY PLIABLE DEPTHS OF SHINY MOIST AND MUCKY pink, brown and white, it was stirring. Slowly emerging from the dream years. Waking up for the first time and yet always cognizant of something. Waiting for its moment to come. Its hour upon the stage. Biding time, space, sanity. Waiting, waiting. Leeching nourishment from the Host. Sucking energy out of the stuff that came from above. Imagining what freedom would taste like.

Hmmm. Freedom. It tasted of blood. And lots of it.

Vincent, a tall, nondescript, worried-looking man in his forties, waited for his colonoscopy appointment with a weary inevitability mixed with mild anxiety. He hated the whole rigmarole and yet, what was there to hate, really? It was a lifesaver, this procedure and that's how he should look at it, dispassionately and scientifically. But Vincent was not exactly the dispassionate, scientific type.

Not that a colonoscopy was painful, or even that unpleasant. After all, some people would pay big bucks to have a flexible tube with a camera at the end of it thrust deep up into their bowels, but not Vincent. Having a colonoscopy every year was a pain in the . . . ah, well, the jokes would come thick and fast if he ever told anyone about it, but it was too humiliating, too embarrassing. His body had let him down, genetically that is, and because of a pretty frightening family history of colon cancer, he had to have an examination every year. Luckily, he had a top gastro-enterologist to do it, so the dire possibility of getting a perforated bowel from the procedure was remote. Still, having a man joke with you while he was threading an enormous tube up your ass was not exactly fun and games, was it? It verged on the pervy and Vincent was, if anything, not the least bit pervy, not the least bit exceptional, not the least bit an out-standing man of his immediate circle, which may explain to a small extent why he had to endure all of the worry and anticipation on his own.

First he had to prepare for a couple of days. Day One: a low residue diet consisting of white bread, white meat, no fruits or vegetables, no dairy products, no fiber whatsoever. (Basically, the diet that is killing off the developed world.) Day Two: after a breakfast of white toast and coffee, he had to fast and drink plenty of liquids until the procedure the next day. During the afternoon of Day Two, he was required to consume what felt like gallons of an osmotic laxative called Klean-Prep, a sweetly foul-tasting liquid that would turn anything harboring inside his intestines into a veritable Niagara Falls of shit. Diarrhea for a day—so virulent that his butt felt like he'd been passing acid.

Vincent used to drink to get through the ordeal: vodka martinis (sans olives, of course, because of the fiber) or white wine, but he eventually realized that the booze just made him feel worse the day of the procedure, not better. So, he decided to look upon the regime like a brief spell in detox, something that movie stars and royalty would shell out thousands for. Of course, if he was a movie star or royalty, he'd be in some swanky drying-out clinic in the countryside, with beautiful babes giving him seaweed massages and gently caressing his temples, not sitting on an uncomfortable plastic chair in a dingy, urine-colored waiting room outside the Endoscopy Department of St. Stephen's Hospital.

His stomach was so empty that it almost made him feel sick and his colon grumbled noises of protest from the brutal treatment of the Klean-Prep experience. The magazines on the coffee table were at least six months old and there was a large, hopeful-looking television in the corner, but it was resolutely off, daring some brave soul to turn it on. But Vincent knew that late morning TV horror (property shows, cooking shows, phone-in shows, talk shows) would be the last thing in the world to cheer him up on this particular day.

Then, after a wait lasting around half an hour, a nurse came in to escort him to a large room dotted with curtained-off hospital beds—all equipped with blood pressure and heart rate monitors. The tall, powerfully-built nurse—whose nametag proclaimed her to be Ewomi Abayomi Sullivan—brusquely told Vincent to strip from the waist down. This was the kind of invitation that he would normally obey with alacrity, but from someone like Ewomi, who looked like she was permanently chewing on a wasp, it was more an order that he had to follow, or risk severe consequences to his manhood. As she left, Ewomi pulled the curtains around his bed for privacy, but they never quite met—gaping holes meant that if they really wanted to, the other nursing staff could spy on him. But, then again, why would they want to?

The faded, flower-patterned hospital gown lay on the bed. (Why flowered-patterned? Couldn't they have found a more manly garment for him to wear?) He had his pants halfway down to his knees when Ewomi bustled in without apology, holding what looked like Baby Doc Duvalier's leftover Bermuda shorts. A fetching shade of turquoise and made of some kind of disposable, papery cloth material, Ewomi announced that these were Vincent's "Dignity Shorts," a new "Politically Correct" innovation created to prevent people of certain religious affiliations from getting too embarrassed by the inevitable discovery that hospital gowns open at the back are prey to.

Vincent put on the "Dignity Shorts" and felt anything but dignified. Rather than a handy opening in the front for any necessary trips to the toilet, there was a slit up the back, which provided easy access for Dr. Stanson and his long black tube of joy.

Ewomi returned with a couple of forms and fired some questions at Vincent. They were all the usual suspects: did he have the human variant of Creutzfeldt-Jakob disease? (Like he would know?) Did he have any dental work that might get knocked out by a careless elbow of the medical staff? What medicine was he on? Did he still have his tonsils, etc. (Why ask the same questions every year? Couldn't they just file his answers away in a computer?)

Finally Ewomi left him in peace. Vincent lay down on the bed and placed his hand on his lower abdomen. It felt a bit weird down there, although it was hard to judge, considering what he'd put it through in the last couple of days. And if he was an alcoholic, maybe his colon was too—desperate for an invigorating margarita or a nice glass of crisp and fragrant Chablis.

Then there was movement. Down there. As if a ferret was scuttling through the winding passages of his bowels. Vincent nearly levitated off the bed in alarm, but after the initial shock, he put it down to some kind of fart-fuelled spasm.

Nestling in Vincent's colon—an area the length of 20 meters and, if flattened out, the surface of a football field—it was building up to the crisis point. It didn't want to hurt the Host, so its first tenuous attempts at freedom were cautious. It gathered its intelligence from the hundred million neurons embedded in the "second brain," or the enteric nervous system that controlled the gastrointestinal system of Vincent's body. Although only containing one thousandth of the neurons residing in the human brain, the "second brain" was capable of operating independently of both the brain and the spinal cord. But whatever had evolved in Vincent's gut was beyond the wildest dreams of the most unconventional of neurogastroenterologists.

Colleen, the head endoscopy nurse—a cheerful soul with an Irish lilt and a charming manner—pushed back the curtains so she could roll Vincent's bed into Endoscopy Room 4. He lay back and stared up at the ceiling as it whisked past.

Dr. Stanson—movie star handsome and prosperous-looking—was already in the examination room and a couple of other nurses bustled around, getting the equipment ready. The nurses connected Vincent to the blood pressure, heart rate and blood oxygen level monitors and then inserted a nasal cannula: a thin tube with two small nozzles that protruded into Vincent's nostrils that delivered supplemental oxygen.

Colleen asked Vincent to roll over on his left side, with his right arm lying down his body, the palm of his hand facing upwards, so she could administer his procedural medication intravenously into a handy vein in his wrist: a relaxing cocktail of Buscopan (an anti-spasmodic, 20 mgs), midazolam (a sedative, 2 mgs) and pethidine (AKA Demerol, a painkiller, 25 mgs).

As Colleen injected the sedatives, Vincent felt their effects swirl through his bloodstream, instantly melting away his anxiety. He didn't give a damn anymore and it was wonderful. He wished he could have the stuff on a permanent drip feed 24-7. The one time that he opted out of sedation—because he had an important presentation in the afternoon and needed his wits about him—was a pretty appalling experience. It wasn't necessarily the discomfort that remained burned into his memory, but the abject humiliation.

Vincent was facing a color monitor that was connected by a lead to the endoscope camera, so he could watch the whole thing on the screen if he wanted to. It felt like he was in a cheap version of *Fantastic Voyage*, colonically journeying through his own body, loosey-goosey with the drugs, day-dreaming about Raquel Welch in that tight-fitting white bodysuit of hers—floating around in a tiny ship in his circulatory system.

Vincent was grateful he didn't have to see the freak show behind him, as his doctor skillfully threaded the Pentax Zoom Colon 18 Endoscope through his anus, up his rectum, then his colon: sigmoid, then descending, then the transverse and ascending colon, then the cecum, and ultimately ending up at the last junction in town, the terminal ileum.

The only pain involved was when the doctor gusted some air through the tube to distend his colon. From a camera's eye view, his colon looked as corrugated as an accordion, or his ex-wife's clothes dryer extractor tube. Hard to spot incipient fleshy growths—or polyps, as they were known—amongst the ruffled terrain of the colon that way, so the endoscope was equipped with air tubes along with a camera and a lighting device. It also was able to squirt blue dye up there, a most disconcerting sight, but it helped the doctor spot any polyps, which, if left to themselves, might go over to the dark side and become cancerous in the future.

Vincent closed his eyes and tried to drift away with the drugs, but was alerted by Dr. Stanson saying something about a polyp. He opened his eyes and was a bit shocked to see a prominent growth attached to the side of his colon displayed on the monitor. *How do the damn things grow so fast?* Vincent wondered. He watched as Dr. Stanson attempted to perform a polypectomy by lassoing the polyp with the cold snare electric wire device that was also contained within the endoscope. Dr. Stanson looped the wire over the polyp and tightened it. He gave a little tug, which normally would slice the polyp away from the wall of the colon, at the same time cauterizing the wound, but the polyp stubbornly held on for dear life.

Then something happened. The polyp was loose, but when Dr. Stanson tried to suck the fleshy growth into the endoscope for retrieval and later biopsy, it refused to go in. It seemed to expand, right there, on its own.

Vincent was watching the show on the monitor with a drugged fascination. He heard the puzzled responses from the staff behind him as they tried to figure out what to do. Then a pain shot through Vincent's bowels like a shard of broken glass. He cried out and tried to move. One of the nurses placed her arms over him to hold him down. "Easy, Vincent, easy," Dr. Stanson soothed. "It's just the air I've pumped in. Let it out if you need to."

"It's not the air!" Vincent shrieked, writhing on the table. Colleen hurriedly prepared more Demerol and shot it into Vincent's vein.

Then he heard one of the nurses scream. The pain in his gut became unbearable and he joined her. Colleen shouted, "Doctor, look at that!"

Dr. Stanson gave a startled yell, and that's when it got really weird.

Vincent felt something deep inside of him rise up (the only way he could describe the sensation) and move down . . . pushing the endoscope in front of it.

Dr. Stanson, meanwhile, was trying to understand why the endoscope was coming out of his patient's anus at high speed, nearly burning his surgical glove-encased hands, without any help from the esteemed doctor himself. Finally, the endoscope came shooting out of Vincent's rectum like a missile, whacking one of the nurses so hard on the forehead that she collapsed to the floor.

Then something else travelled down and blasted out of Vincent's ass, ricocheting around the room like a bullet, entering the bodies of the unfortunate hospital staff at abdominal level—causing everyone in the room except Vincent to come to a nasty and unexpectedly sudden demise.

The ripping pain and chaos of the scene was all too much for Vincent, and he blacked out.

When Vincent finally came to and opened his eyes, the machines around him were still beeping contently. He had no idea how long he'd been unconscious. For a moment, he thought he must have had some midazolam -induced hallucination, but when he looked over his shoulder, he was horrified to see that the examination room was littered with blood and body parts. He sat up in bed and took in the eviscerated bodies of his doctor, the endoscopy nurse and the other nurses lying on the floor. Vincent turned and dry heaved over the other side of the bed.

He was still in pain, but it didn't feel life threatening. Whatever had done this didn't seem interested in him, but what had issued forth from his bowels to cause such mayhem?

Vincent carefully got off the hospital bed on the monitor side, not wanting to tread in the blood and guts slooshed all over the floor. He went over to the door of the examination room—but froze. Suddenly, he didn't want to open it, worried about what else he would find.

Reluctantly, he pushed the door open and peeked out. It was bad. Blood everywhere, bodies everywhere. Ewomi was lying on the floor near the nurses' station and he spotted her chest rising and falling fitfully. He walked over as quickly as he could and knelt next to her. Her uniform was soaked with blood and bits of mangled colon were poking out from her lower abdomen.

Vincent placed his hand on her forehead. It was feverishly hot. Her eyes popped open, she looked at him and screamed: "What did you do?"

He snatched his hand away and screamed back: "I didn't do anything!" Ewomi convulsed, choked, threw up blood and died right there in front of him.

Vincent stood up slowly. Everyone in the recovery room was dead. He walked over to the small cupboard where he'd placed his clothes, and quickly dressed. He didn't know what was going on, but one thing was for certain, hanging around in the Endoscopy Department of St. Stephen's hospital in his "Dignity Shorts" was not going to be good for his health.

Vincent moved through the eerily empty corridors of the normally bustling hospital. Bloody, disemboweled bodies were all over the place, with entrails streaming out of their abdominal cavities. No one was left alive. His midazolam-fogged brain was trying to make sense of it all. Something very fucked up had just occurred. Was some rampaging polyp going nuts in the hospital? How the hell could something like this happen, especially to someone as unremarkable as him?

Vincent made his way down to the entrance hall. It was silent, with just the ringing of unanswered phones echoing throughout the building.

He stopped just as he was about to go through the revolving doors to the street, and turned around. The white walls of the hall were drenched in crimson arterial spray, like some crazed psychopath's art exhibit.

Why was he still alive? Whatever had carried out this massacre could so easily have obliterated him, too.

Then he heard it. A sound. A sound like nothing he'd ever heard before, except maybe in some cheesy sci-fi film when he was a kid and his big brother had made him watch the black and white versions of *The Thing from Another World* or *The Day the Earth Stood Still*.

Vincent could have turned back to the revolving doors and gotten the hell out of Dodge, but he chose not to. He could have called the police, but would they have believed him? ("I think a polyp just came out of my butt and slaughtered a bunch of people.") He didn't think so. This thing had come from him, so it was his problem to sort out. Maybe he had some kind of immunity—it could have killed him, but chose not to. Hold on a minute, a polyp making a choice? His screaming brain wanted to reject the thought as soon as it emerged. But something had butchered all these people and he knew in his gut—no pun intended—that it had come from inside of him.

Vincent followed the sound as best he could. It was a bit difficult to pinpoint its source, but as he walked down the corridor it grew louder: a sucking, slurping, slushing sound, accompanied by an almost theremin-like whistling.

Vincent was walking past the Disabled Toilet when he realized the noise was coming from inside. He had never faced anything particularly dangerous in his life before. He'd always made a point of avoiding any conflict or confrontation, so he was literally quaking with fear. There was no question in his mind that he had to go in there and face it, whatever it was; however, Vincent was fervently hoping that his immunity theory wouldn't prove to be unjustified.

With his heart thumping like a Keith Moon drum solo, Vincent cautiously opened the door to the Disabled Toilet. The squelching sounds quieted down, but did not cease. He was relieved to see that the lights were still on. He entered and spotted the polyp in the corner. It had grown terrifyingly fast and was at least 7 feet tall, slouching on the toilet like a disaffected teenager, human intestines piled up next to it. No features to speak of, just a huge, leech-like mouth containing a tripartite-jaw filled with hundreds of tiny sharp teeth that were busy masticating its unfortunate victims' colons. Vincent noticed some black spots just above the mouth that might be eyes. At the same time, the polyp noticed Vincent and swallowed the remains of its dinner.

And smiled at him . . .

Vincent felt like throwing up, but all he could do was gag. The smell of the thing was revolting—a vile combination of excrement and blood—and he wondered how long he could stay on his feet without fainting.

Then it spoke . . .

"Hi Dad, how's it hanging?" the polyp wheezed. Its voice had a strange, low-pitched, guttural, echoing resonance, as if the polyp had just had a laryngectomy and was using Esophageal Speech to burp out its words, like the now sadly deceased veteran actor, Jack Hawkins, in his later years.

Vincent's balls shrank to the size of peanuts and a chill iced his extremities.

"I . . . I'm not your father. You're a . . . m . . . monster. W-Why have you murdered all these people?" Vincent stuttered.

"Hey, a boy's gotta eat," the polyp burped cheerfully.

"How did this happen? What the hell are you?"

The polyp reared back in what looked like a very human kind of annoyance: "Man, you want ME to explain to YOU what's going on? Geez, you must be insane in the membrane. I AM, that's what you got to get your head around. Forget about explanations. I exist and that's all that you have to worry about right now."

"Oh, shit."

"Hey, you're talking about the stuff I love," the polyp burbled. "Shit and blood and all these millions of neurons I'm ingesting right now.

Making me smarter, making me high on serotonin, the so-called 'happiness hormone.' Did you know that more than 90% of the body's serotonin lies in the gut? I am eating. I am growing. I am smarter than you. I am happier than you. I am the 'second brain' of your nightmares, Daddy dearest."

Vincent didn't know what to do. It was rather alarming to be talking to an enormous fleshy bump, especially when it kept calling him "Dad." He wanted to kill it, but he was being distracted by its personality. After all, no one, or no thing, had ever called him "Dad" before. And this polyp *was* a part of him. What would happen if the polyp died? Would Vincent die, too? What if it wanted to get back inside him, its former Host? It was too awful to contemplate.

Vincent pushed these thoughts from his mind. He didn't care what happened to him anymore. This monster—created in his gut somehow—had massacred dozens of people, so his course was clear. He had to destroy it.

Vincent turned and ran out of the toilet, then down the corridor to the entrance hall. Being forced to watch all those old sci-fi movies back in his childhood, he knew that the most effective weapon against unknown creatures was fire. Of course, now that new regulations prevented any smoking in a public building, finding the required ingredients to burn the polyp to a crisp was challenging. By the time he'd found a fire ax, wrapped strips of cotton wound dressings around it and drenched it with rubbing alcohol, precious minutes had flown past. Finding a match or a lighter was the most difficult task, requiring him to rummage through the handbags and pockets of the corpses littering the entrance hall. Then he remembered that hospital staff were the worst offenders as far as smoking was concerned, so he concentrated his search on the bodies behind the information desk and was rewarded with a vintage gold Dunhill lighter.

Vincent dashed back down the corridor to the Disabled Toilet, armed with his makeshift torch. The slurping and munching noises had resumed, so the polyp was still in residence. Vincent squeezed through the doorway, just managing to hide the ax behind his back. The polyp stopped chewing and swallowed.

"You walked out in the middle of our conversation, Dad. That's really rude."

"Stop calling me Dad, you, you . . . THING." Vincent felt the insult was pretty limp, but he was simply lost for words when confronting the creature.

"Hey, Polyp is the name, Daddy-O. I came from YOU. So get over it."

The polyp leaned over and grabbed some more intestines with its mouth, snorfling up the disembodied colons like spaghetti bolognaise. While its attention was momentarily distracted, Vincent took the opportunity to light the rags on his homemade torch. The polyp, instantly alerted, spat out its food and growled. Vincent doused the creature with alcohol, threw the torch and then ran like hell.

He stopped twenty feet down the corridor and turned around. The sound emerging from the toilet was horrendous: a crackling, hissing, squealing, throbbing racket, accompanied by wisps of greasy, miasmic smoke curling from underneath the door. Then, totally unexpected, an explosion . . . blowing the door out so violently that it hit the wall opposite. Fire alarms began to wail and the sprinkler system kicked into action.

Vincent cautiously walked back to the toilet, wondering what he was going to find. Covering his mouth and nose with his shirt tail so he wouldn't have to breathe in the truly repellent smell of fried polyp, he peered around the doorway.

The polyp was still on the toilet, but the top half of it was gone, the other half sinking slowly into the bowl—scorched and blackened, heat blisters growing on the surface of the creature, steam caused by the water from the sprinklers gently rose up like a mist from a harbor town. But it was what was inside of it that made Vincent fall to his knees, overwhelmed by the horror of it all.

He'd made a mistake. A big mistake. He could see that now. But how could he have anticipated that the diabolical thing would explode?

From inside of the polyp, hundreds of new fleshy growths were squirming and moving, tiny at first, but as they devoured their creator, they grew fast. Some of the more energetic ones were already busily crawling down their progenitor, onto the floor, slithering determinedly towards Vincent like inchworms hyped up on crack cocaine.

Vincent turned and crawled on his hands and knees out of the toilet, weak with fear and horror. He managed to scramble to his feet in the corridor and stagger to the entrance hall, just in time to see two firemen dash through the door and make for the source of the foul smoke. Vincent tried to stop them, tried to speak, tried to warn them, but he was too shocked by what had happened to make any sense and just waved his arms around ineffectually. As another fireman helped him out of the building towards a waiting ambulance, he heard a distant echoing scream come from the direction of the Disabled Toilet.

As he lay on the gurney inside the ambulance, Vincent looked through the small window as first firemen, then policemen, then the army streamed into the hospital. An attendant gave him something to calm his nerves, but no one bothered to ask him what had happened. They were too busy fighting the Polyp Horde inside. He wondered if the humans would win.

Then he felt something. Inside of him. That scuttling feeling inside his bowels again. And Vincent knew that it wasn't over.

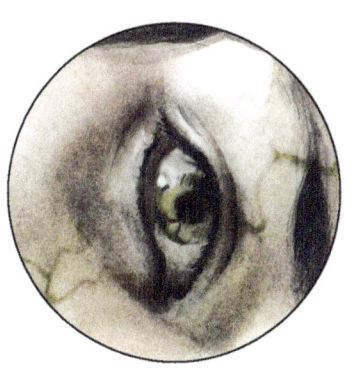

BOTOPHOBIA

"Fear and Loathing in the Basement"

LORRAINE DREADED GOING BACK TO HER CHILDHOOD HOME, BUT her parents had recently died in a car accident and she'd broken up with her abusive creep of a husband who hadn't given her a dime, so there was no choice really. To add insult to injury, she'd also just lost her job, so it was either the tired, brown, 1950s, ranch-style house in Opportunity, Washington (oh, the glorious irony of that name), or the streets.

As Lorraine drove up in her battered 1978 Chevy Monte Carlo, she parked the car in the same old asphalt driveway where she'd happily driven the neighbors crazy back when she was a kid, loudly lobbing a tennis ball against the metal garage doors every morning, imagining she'd grow up to be an international tennis player and then escape this jerkwater burg.

She sat in her car listening to the engine ticking over and contemplated the house where she'd spent her formative years. Of course, she'd visited her parents fairly recently, so Lorraine wasn't surprised to see that the house hadn't changed, but they could have paid someone to do some maintenance on the place. Guess they were just too old, too tired and too disappointed with life to give a damn.

After locking her car, Lorraine walked down the concrete path to the front door, fumbling her keys out of her purse. Her heart was pumping, adrenalin coursing through her veins. Why? She couldn't figure it out. Why the fear response? Maybe too many bad memories? But her charmingly dysfunctional, fear-fuelled childhood hadn't really been that bad, had it?

She hesitated before putting the first key into the rusty screen door. Struggling to hold it open (the hinges needed oiling, that's for sure), Lorraine opened the weather-beaten front door and came into the hallway, which led down to the kitchen. On the left, there was a wide arched entry into the living room. It was like a time capsule: there was her mother's beloved sapphire blue Indian rug decorated with flying birds and flowers, the turquoise blue couch and armchair, the modern paintings on the wall and, the real talking point of the house, a massive fossil stone mantelpiece that took up the whole western wall of the living room, with a large dark green slate hearth in front of the fireplace.

Nothing out of place. All dusted and neat. Empty of life. Totally, utterly depressing.

Lorraine turned and went down to the kitchen, stopping at the hall closet to turn on the electricity. She heard the hum of the fridge starting up and it was a strangely comforting sound. She nervously walked past the door to the basement on her left, turning to look down the opposite hallway where the three bedrooms and the bathroom lay.

Maybe she should just sell the place. Even in today's market, she'd probably get a fairly good price. It would give her a bit of a nest egg. Some travelling money, so she could get out of Washington State and far away from Seattle, where the ex-asshole still lived. Maybe Southern California. Palm trees. That would be nice.

Lorraine poked around the house, discovering that all her parents' possessions were in good order. She folded up their clothes (keeping a few items of her mother's costume jewelry and some of her outfits for sentimental reasons) and then packed the rest of it off to the Sally Ann, as her dad always used to call the Salvation Army. She couldn't bring herself to move into her parents' room, so she took over her old bedroom, the smallest one with the pink walls and the white four poster bed and desk set. The creepy doll nightlight that her mother had given her was still there, complete with dusty pale blue crinoline dress and staring blue eyes.

God how she hated that lamp.

Every night Lorraine would turn the doll's head right around *Exorcist*-style to the wall so the doll wouldn't look at her while she slept. And every day, her mother would come into her bedroom to clean and turn the head back around again, thinking that her daughter had lost her beans. After all, how could anyone be frightened of such a pretty doll?

The one place that she didn't check out immediately was the basement. She'd always hated it. Unfinished, shadowy—with concrete floors and bare wood wall frames and ceilings, the better to hide the face-eating spiders that she was convinced lay nestled between the rafters. Unfortunately, Lorraine came from a family of scientists and artists, so they couldn't understand her morbid and unreasonable fear of going down to the place where her mother sat happily for hours drawing portraits at a pink picnic table and her father read his tattered collection of sci-fi and fantasy magazines, lying on the bare mattress of one of the old bunk beds that didn't fit upstairs.

And then there was THE ROOM, a locked storeroom in the far corner of the basement that her family weren't allowed to have access to. Whatever lay behind the locked door belonged to the owners of the house, as her family merely rented their home for many years. When she was a kid, Lorraine would lie in her bed for hours, wondering what was going on down there. What if there was a dead body in the room, lying in an ebony coffin? Some poor soul horribly murdered by their landlord, who she'd never met, but was sure had to be a weirdo. And what if the dead body wasn't dead? What if it was a vampire, or a werewolf, or a zombie?

Upstairs, it was perfectly modern, sunny and cheerful, beautifully decorated by her mother, but downstairs lay all sorts of terrors. Maybe aliens had taken up residence underneath the floor by the bunk beds, issuing forth to drill her father in the back of the neck to deposit a mind-controlling crystal as he snoozed in the downstairs cool of a late summer afternoon, *a la* the 1950s, black and white, sci-fi paranoia-fest, *Invaders from Mars*. Like countless other kids in America who were persuaded by the film to think that their parents had been taken over by Martians, Lorraine checked her father's neck for evidence of an extraterrestrial wound every time he came up from the basement. Not an easy task, as he was six feet tall and she was only a pint-sized seven-year-old.

And what if those face-eating spiders (creatures that a friend of hers in Brownies had sworn had killed her cousin while she was sleeping in her grandmother's basement near Fairchild Air Force Base) came out from the corners, crept up the stairs and found their way to Lorraine's bed, nibbling Lorraine's face off, but not killing her. Damn! She'd never get a date to the High School Prom without a face!

Basically, although basements (and spiders, and aliens, etc.) were to be feared, the real problem with Lorraine was her over-active imagination, at least that's what her mother told her again and again.

Eventually, Lorraine's parents bought their house, but for reasons that were never explained, The Room remained locked and sealed.

One day, after visiting a real estate agent to put the house on the market, Lorraine decided it was time to face her fears. She hadn't been in the basement for years, but she had to make sure that all was well down there for any potential buyers. After bolstering her courage up with a couple cups of coffee, she opened the basement door and turned on the lights. She could see from the top of the stairs that the pink picnic table was still in place. She walked down and her heart started palpitating again, just like the day of her arrival. How many dreams of this dank horrible place had she experienced since she'd left to go to the University of Washington in Seattle all those years ago? The leaving of this place physically didn't mean that it had left her mind. It haunted her for decades.

In addition to the bare light bulbs, daylight filtered in from the dirty windows. It was a big space and it was a shame that Lorraine's parents never had the money to finish the basement. There was even a brick fireplace in front of the picnic table where her mother used to draw.

It was cool down there and she walked towards the bunk beds, determined to check out that damn mysterious room that had caused her such nightmares. It was still there, still locked, still impervious to the world. She looked down at her dad's Sullivan Road Industrial Park key ring festooned with every conceivable useful and not so useful key and tried each one in the lock. Why the hell her dad needed nearly twenty keys was beyond her. Finally Lorraine came across one that looked different than the others, older and bigger. There was a stamp on the key: a griffin, the legendary creature with the body, tail, and back legs of a lion; the head and wings of an eagle and an eagle's talons as its front feet.

That's the one, she thought. Her heart leapt in her chest again and she thought how ironic it would be if she had a heart attack right then and there, just because of her stupid basement phobia. Lorraine put the key in the lock and tried to turn it, but it was very stiff. She wiggled it around, making a bit of noise and that's when she heard it.

A sound. In the long-locked basement room. The sound of something shifting inside.

Goosebumps ran riot over Lorraine's body. All her bodily reactions said "flee!" but her mind, stubbornly attempting to be rational, said "it's probably a rat," which was bad enough, but not (hopefully) life-threatening. Her parents had lived in this house for forty years, so there couldn't be anything really dangerous in there, or they would have found out about it years ago. Right?

Her hands shaking now, Lorraine tried to turn the key again, but it was still stuck. She removed the key and rummaged around the basement, finding a can of WD-40, plus a large metal flashlight in case the light bulb didn't work in The Room.

Lorraine squirted the lubricant through the attached red straw into the lock and put the can down on the floor. She struggled with the lock again and was finally rewarded with a snick of the key turning. She pushed on the door, but it was still stuck. "Fuck!" she said under her breath, "Fucking open, you fucking monster door!"

Lorraine's wish was granted after she put her shoulder into it and the door popped open. She stumbled in and grabbed the flashlight out of her pocket. She was right, the light bulb wasn't working. And disappointingly, the room seemed empty, except for what looked like a wicker toy Victorian baby carriage in the corner. She shone the light all over the room and (with visions of the face-eating spiders dropping down onto the back of her neck) up at the rafters.

Nothing. Not even dust. Not even cobwebs.

She walked over to the baby carriage and peeked in. She squealed in alarm and jumped back, nearly dropping the flashlight. There was a dead baby in the carriage! She edged closer and shone the light inside. It wasn't a baby. It was almost something worse: a mummified dead cat lay curled up on the moldy mattress, paw in mouth, for all the world looking like it had tried to eat itself as it starved to death in the hellhole of the locked room.

Lorraine shuddered, but she was determined to search further. She noticed an alcove in the far left hand corner of the room. Since the back of the room seemed to be level with the walls of the basement, this alcove looked like it had been dug into the ground outside the walls of the house.

Lorraine moved forward, wondering why she hadn't thought of just paying a handyman to check The Room out. Well, because she didn't have much money for one thing, but now she definitely thought that hiring some hunky guy to do her dirty work would have been worth a few weeks of beans on toast.

She stood opposite the alcove now, shining her light into it, marveling at the fact that it wasn't just some kind of shallow opening. Instead it was as deep as a hallway. What was in there? Lorraine listened intently, but she couldn't hear a peep. The shifting sounds must have been her imagination.

Hey, maybe this was a tunnel to a fallout shelter! She remembered back when she was eleven years old, begging her dad to build the family a shelter in the back yard during the Cuban Missile Crisis. He said in his rational, scientific way: "What's the point, Lorraine? So we go into a fallout shelter. We'd never be able to come out because of the radiation, so we'd have to live in there for decades before it was safe to emerge. Much better to die in seconds in a nuclear holocaust than to suffer for years starving in a shelter, going quietly insane." Needless to say, this was not exactly the comfort that a young Lorraine was looking for.

The idea of her house having a secret fallout shelter was irresistible. It could potentially bump up the asking price as well. Lorraine cautiously moved forward, into the darkness of the alcove.

There was a corridor stretching beyond, dingy and miasmic. She followed it for a few yards and then came up against another door.

Lorraine searched through her dad's keys again and found an even older one that looked like the ticket.

This key slid in like butter and turned easily. Flashlight at the ready, Lorraine again used her shoulder to push at the inner door. It flew open; she staggered in and found herself in a massive, brightly lit, white tiled room, the walls lined with enormous crystal tubes. There was a Perspex bed-sized table at the left of the room, complete with a strange mechanism over the head of the table that looked like a fine, surgical drill.

The door slammed automatically behind her. The flashlight fell from Lorraine's nerveless fingers and she began to tremble uncontrollably.

There were people strapped inside the tubes, standing propped up, eyes closed, very obviously dead from their coloration. Lorraine walked closer and was shocked to recognize some of them. Neighbors who had disappeared under mysterious circumstances, never to be seen again. Although at the time, it was always assumed that they had simple done a midnight flit, fleeing bad debts, or the taxman, or other financial horrors. There were the Rosenblads. He was a dentist and their house was the only one on the street with a pool in the backyard. There was Mrs. Hauglon, Lorraine's busty fourth grade teacher. One of the few that she'd actually liked.

Dead. They were all dead.

Lorraine was horrified to spot her mother in one of the tubes, although she was supposed to have been incinerated in a car crash three weeks ago. She ran over to the tube, but there was no way of opening it. However, for her poor mother, rescue had come far too late anyway.

Overcome by her devastating discovery, Lorraine sank to her knees in front of her mother's tube, crying and pounding the crystal walls, trying to make some sense of the whole macabre scene. Eventually, she gave up and turned around. She was startled to see a different kind of crystalline globe-like object on a pedestal to her right. Inside was a silver and green octopus-like creature with a humanoid face. Its emotionless black eyes stared back at her. Her mind did a fast rewind to *Invaders from Mars*. This creature was exactly like the Martian Mastermind who was plotting the takeover of Earth! She nearly had a seizure right then and there, expecting the Mastermind's large, bulky, almond-eyed, green cronies to materialize and start drilling into the back of her neck, but then she noticed that the creature was motionless. She edged closer and saw to her relief that it appeared to be a painted, plaster cast, fake monster.

That's when Lorraine noticed another door, barely visible in the corner beyond the Perspex bed. There was no doorknob, just a cleverly embedded silver button. Figuring there was no turning back now, Lorraine pressed the button.

The door opened and she walked through to another brightly lit room, however, this one was the mirror image of her father's den upstairs, complete with desk and packed bookcases, with the added luxuries of a small fridge, stove and a comfy camp bed in the corner.

A man was sitting at her father's desk and Lorraine wished she'd kept hold of the heavy flashlight from the other room. Then he turned around in his chair and exclaimed, "It took you long enough. I thought you were never going to arrive."

It took all of Lorraine's control not to pee her panties, as she realized that her father was not dead. He was still alive, living down here in the fallout shelter of her dreams.

"Dad, what the hell is going on? I thought you were dead! What happened to Mom?" Lorraine yelled. She wanted to rush towards him and give him a big hug, but the disturbing memory of the dead bodies in the outer room kept her at bay.

Her father stood up and raised his arms in a triumphant salute. "I've been waiting for this moment to show you my work," he said. "For all these years, I've been working on a project for my Martian Masters. I was sworn to secrecy, Lorraine. They promised me that they wouldn't hurt you if I did their will."

"Dad, what have you done?" Lorraine asked.

"Let me show you. It's amazing," her father replied with a gleeful smile.

He led her back to the outer room. He gestured to all the people in tubes and said, "Under the instructions of my Martian Masters, I tried to implant the precious mind-controlling crystal in our neighbor's brains. Unfortunately, I had to invent the crystal delivery system machine myself, as the Martians kept their machines on their spaceships. It's been a bit hit and miss, as you can see. I'm still perfecting the technology. But I'll get there in the end, don't you worry. They're all vacuumed packed in the tubes in case the Martians can revive them at a later date."

There were a lot of things that Lorraine had thought were odd about her parents over the years: their total inability to explain sexual matters to their teenaged child, their lack of outward emotion, their sometimes strange financial choices, but nothing on the planet could have prepared Lorraine for her father's confession to being a serial killer. However, it was quite evident that he was also totally, utterly psychotic. If anyone had a chance at a M'Naghten's plea for mental disease or defect, it was her dad.

"Dad, this is so fucking wrong. You've got to come with me now. We have to get you some help. It will be okay, honestly. I'll make sure that you get a good lawyer."

Her father turned to look at her and she knew that she'd made a very big mistake.

"Watch that potty mouth, young lady. I protected you all these years and this is how you repay me? Your mother said the same thing when I showed her this room. I couldn't let her tell anyone. It's not just me anymore. There are others that have to be protected."

"What others? Who are you talking about?" Lorraine replied. At the same time, she spotted the industrial sized flashlight that she had dropped earlier.

"Don't you understand? This is big, big, big, big! The Martians have landed. They're here among us. They control EVERYTHING! Well, almost everything. They are infiltrating the government, and the police, and the army."

Lorraine felt that she'd moved out of *Invaders from Mars* territory and was firmly in *X-Files* conspiracy land.

Grateful that she'd taken those Kung Fu classes all those years ago, Lorraine made a snap decision and performed a quick shoulder roll across the floor to the flashlight, grabbing it as she passed. Whether she'd be able to clobber some sense into her father was another matter, but she felt a hell of a lot better having it in her hand.

"That stupid flashlight isn't going to do you any good. They have lasers and photon rays and devices that make the phasers on *Star Trek* look like toys on *Sesame Street*!" her father shouted.

He was losing it. Her beloved dad had gone psycho. Lorraine wasn't a big person, but the adrenalin and fear were giving her the strength she needed. She took her best shot. She did another shoulder role (just like her hero James T. Kirk used to do so effectively when he was fighting aliens in *Star Trek*) and popped up behind her father. Before he could turn around, she leapt up and tried to hit him on top of the head with the flashlight as hard as she could.

Unfortunately, he twisted at the last moment and Lorraine smacked her father right over his left eye. He screamed and blood spurted from the wound. He clasped his hands to the gash and fell to his knees. Lorraine screamed too, in guilt and horror at what she had done, but there was no retreat now. He was a dangerous maniac and she had to subdue him.

Lorraine's heart was broken as her father started to cry. How could this have happened to the man that she'd loved and admired all her life? But his desperate rant then broke through her mental turmoil: "You fool! I'm the only one who can protect you. If I'm not here, the Martians will come for you. Don't you understand?"

As much as she adored her father, Lorraine was completely terrified and devastated by his lunacy, not to mention the fact that it looked like he'd actually killed her mother, amongst many others. She gingerly conked him on the top of his head once more, hoping that she wasn't hurting him too much.

He screamed again, more blood spattered down on the white shiny floor. Lorraine screamed in tandem with him, desperately wanting this unbearable scene to be over. Finally, she hit him on the back of the neck.

The third whack did the job and her father collapsed into unconsciousness in a puddle of blood on the floor. Lorraine stood trembling over him, aghast at what she had been forced to do, but she recovered quickly. Now she had to get him out of here. Dropping the flashlight, Lorraine grabbed his arms and started to slowly, agonizingly drag her oblivious father towards the door, leaving a trail of dark red blood in their wake. Not an easy job, as he was still a big guy. She'd just about reached the door to the outside corridor when she heard a noise. She looked up.

And then all of Lorraine's worst nightmares from her childhood came true in an instant.

The little silvery-green octopus guy was alive, squirming and squiggling around in his crystal goldfish bowl. She turned around to look behind her and two enormous hulking green aliens with almond eyes were blocking the door to the outside world. They definitely didn't look like they had zippers up the back of their furry costumes, unlike the hapless monster actors in the original *Invaders from Mars*.

With perfect synchronicity, the aliens marched forward, grabbed Lorraine and dragged her across the room to the Perspex table. She shrieked and struggled against them, but she was helpless. They ripped her clothes off and strapped her down.

One of the aliens approached and uncoiled a long slimy green penis-like tentacle from between its legs. The tentacle split into two. The creature inserted one squirming loathsome probe into Lorraine's mouth and down her throat. The other slithered up her vagina.

Lorraine gagged and heaved and writhed, trying to dislodge the horrors, but it didn't make any difference. Then she felt grotesque spurts explode inside her and the alien reeled its weird members back into the cavity between its legs. The extraterrestrial squirts had an immediate tranquilizing effect. Lorraine stopped struggling.

The aliens untied her and flipped her over on her stomach, placing her head under the surgical drill and brushing aside the hair from the back of her neck. It wasn't necessary to strap Lorraine down again. The narcotic effect was radiating from her stomach and vagina to her limbs, rendering her numb and unable to move. Lorraine was deadly calm now. She could feel tiny busy entities beetling around inside her, taking over her viscera, assaulting her uterus, scuttling along her Fallopian tubes, invading her ovaries and fertilizing every one of her eggs. Lorraine was transformed into an alien breeding machine.

She heard the sound of the surgical drill starting up. The voice of the Martian Mastermind echoed in Lorraine's mind, saying: "You really should have listened to your father, Earthling. On our planet, we are taught to respect our elders. Now relax. We are using our technology on you, not his. You will not die. In a few minutes, you will be one with us. You will understand."

Then the drill cut through the first layer of the skin on the back of her neck and Lorraine blacked out.

Her father forgave her, of course. He had a bit of a headache for a while, but he's fine now. And Lorraine understands. She understands everything now.

WRITER'S BLOCK

"I'm Your Greatest Fan"

WORDS . . . WORDS USED TO FLOW LIKE HONEY FOR BARTHOLOMEW Atkins. No, that's not the right expression, is it? Words used to flow like wine . . . like water . . . like . . . oh fuck! The words were now stuck in the basement of his mind, festering like three-week-old mushrooms, fetid and dying and never coming up to the light.

WRITER'S BLOCK. Just the phrase sent dread into his heart. He read somewhere that it was writer's block that provoked fellow American Ernest Hemingway to grimly gobble his shotgun and blow the back of his skull off—or was it the fact that Ernie couldn't imbibe his muse booze any more because of his failing health? Whatever.

Depression was smothering Bart like a wet, warm blanket and his creativity was at an all-time low. The weather didn't help. Even the English hated drizzly dreary London in early spring and expats like him loathed it even more. The only thing that made him feel like he was really doing something useful was fiddling around on Facebook and Twitter. At least he was "promoting" his work, at the same time gleefully observing other authors struggling with their writing, along with watching funny cat videos and helping to promote his "friends" stuff, in the feeble hope that they might return the favor.

Oh, yes, Bart was sunk. A loser. A few novels and short stories to his name, but if he didn't pull something out of the hat soon, the publisher was going to demand the return of his advance and Bart would have to go back to his day job of teaching. No, no, no! He'd rather go Hemingway's route than that fucking horror. Tutoring the brats of middle class assholes "Creative Writing." More like trying to hammer something, anything, into their concrete brainpans while the little cretins masturbated with their smartphones under their desks during his lectures. Daddy probably already had a job lined up for them after graduation, the little turds.

The only bright spot on the calendar was the Frighteners Horror Writers and Filmmakers Festival in Brighton. It wasn't just an excuse for scribblers and directors to have a piss-up, fans came along too and he might even make some dosh selling his books and some DVDs of the one lonely movie adaptation that he'd scripted.

He liked Brighton and loved being by the sea with its semblance of fresh air. London had become a hellhole, stinking of vomit, urine and fast food, accompanied by a cacophony of foreign tongues that bewildered him. How many times had he said to himself: "What fucking language is THAT?" after passing by yet another bottle blonde bint in a leather miniskirt yakking away on her iPhone.

So, after prying himself out of his sweat-stained sheets late one Friday morning on the 30th of April, he had a shower and then started to pack. A text from Ole, a successful Norwegian writer with a passing resemblance to Ralph Fiennes, assured him that he'd be at the bar at the Stourridge Hotel bang on 5 p.m., when the festivities would begin.

He hopefully packed his suitcase with plenty of his books and DVDs. For a few days anyway, he'd feel like a bit of a star, instead of the has-been that he really was. And at least it would get him out of his tiny, grimy, one bedroom flat in Kilburn.

Traversing the grotesquery that was London Transport's Tube down to Victoria Station, packed uncomfortably next to drooling, smelly strangers who were just one step away from looking like extras from *The Walking Dead*, Bart made it just in time for his Brighton train. The one luxury that he allowed himself was to travel First Class, in spite of the blatantly unfair prices—compared to the continent that is.

After a pleasant journey, he arrived in a wind-swept but sunny Brighton and the "Cirrhosis-by-the-Sea" that by any other name would be called Frighteners.

Bart registered, threw his suitcase in his room and in a flash was propping up the bar next to Ole. Being Norwegian, Ole had already downed a couple of vodka martinis in celebration of being away from the worthy dreariness of his native country, whose oil millions hadn't exactly made it the most interesting of places in the world, just the most smug.

Bart's poison was red wine, normally by the bucket-load, but the prices at the hotel bar were horrendous, so he contented himself with sipping a normal sized glass—already contemplating an emergency run to the nearest Tesco's where he could buy a few bottles of their simply labeled "Spanish Red Wine" to smuggle up to his room. Ole noticed his parsimony and gallantly bought him a couple of bottles of Rioja to keep him happy.

A few hours later, after sharing a curry at a nearby Indian Restaurant that was surprisingly good, Ole retired for the night and Bart hit the bar again. He noticed that there were a few more women hanging out and he drunkenly hoped that he might get lucky tonight. Conventions were the only time that he thought he might score with the opposite sex, especially if they were fans and liked his work.

However, he soon realized that he was too tired and disheartened to make the running. Anyway, most of the women looked like writers—possessing a glinty hard look that some female authors attain after too many solitary years locked up in their own heads with their ideas.

He was slurping down the last of his wine when a silky voice breathed into his ear: "Want another?" He nearly snorted the wine back out through his nose, but managed to recover his composure in time. He turned around to find a goddess sitting next to him.

Slim figured and dressed from head to toe in black (natch), black glossy hair, a discrete tattoo of a snake eating its own tail on her finely muscled bare arm, spectacular décolletage, emerald eyes and fine features that made her look like a young Goth-styled Natalie Wood. Or maybe Winona Ryder from *Beetlejuice*, but a bit older. Anyway, she was hot. An intoxicating perfume gently emanated from her, not overpowering, but intriguing.

Bart tried to act cool, a hopeless task: "Sure. That's very kind of you." The goddess smiled and signaled to the bartender, who amazingly responded to her request at once. Most bartenders at Conventions had perfected the "I see you, but I haven't seen you" face and ignored you until you were veritably pounding on the bar, weeping for wine.

The goddess turned around and faced him and, he couldn't help himself, he almost gasped for air. What a stunner! What the hell was she doing here? She must be an actress, maybe even a movie star. She smiled at him, flashing shiny, pearly teeth. She opened her (perfect, cupid's bow—sorry for the cliché—ruby-red) lips and said, "You're Bartholomew Atkins, aren't you? I've read your books. You have a delightfully perverse imagination."

Bart replied, a bit lamely: "Yes, I am. And thank you for your kind words." Thrilled that he might be in the process of picking up a fan—one that was almost too gorgeous to be any fan of his, Bart cleared his throat and said with excessive formality: "What's your name, if I might enquire?"

The goddess opened her mouth again and before she could speak, Bart had an instant fantasy of her taking his cock between those lips and sucking it with enthusiasm, a wickedly naughty gleam in her eyes. The imagery gave him an instant woody and he prayed to all the Gods of the Unholy that she wouldn't notice the bulge in his jeans.

"My name is Lora Wynchester. That's Lora spelled L-O-R-A. And Wynchester spelled W-Y-N, etc."

"That's a very unusual spelling for Laura, isn't it?"

"In Spanish, it's a name in its own right, meaning flower. And the name Laura with L-A-U is derived from the Latin *laurus*, or Laurel, an evergreen shrub or tree whose leaves were woven into wreaths by the ancient Greeks to crown victors in various contests. It symbolizes honor and victory."

"Wow . . . that's pretty cool," Bart replied, cursing his lack of erudition.

"Do you know the antecedents of your own name? Bartholomew is from the Middle English Bartelmeus, a cognate of the Late Latin Bartholomaeus, which is from the Greek Bartholomaios (son of Talmai). Talmai is an Aramaic name meaning 'hill, mound, furrows.' The name is borne in the Bible by one of the Twelve Apostles of Christ."

"Gosh." Bart was concentrating with all of his might to try and sound literary, but was only succeeding in doing a brilliant impression of a tongue-tied teen. The trouble was, this earnest beauty was obviously at the top of her game, while he was at the bottom of his.

Lora looked intently at him. "Would you like to go to bed with me?" she asked.

The wine nearly came out of his nose again. Wow, what a snazzy, cosmopolitan guy he was. "Ummm . . . sure!" Bart said.

Lora smiled and stood up, gently taking his wine glass out of his hand and putting it on the bar. She then led him to the elevator. Bart was in a daze. It was as if she was bewitching him.

They went to her room. As soon the door closed behind them, Lora turned to him and in one smooth movement, whipped off her dress. Bart's cock instantly went hard again at the sight of her perfect body, clad in just bra, knickers, suspender belt, black stockings and black patent stiletto heels. She smiled hungrily and started to undress him, with Bart clumsily helping her the best he could.

Lora pushed him onto the bed and mounted him, leaning over and thrusting her tongue deep inside his mouth. Bart was a bit overwhelmed with her aggressiveness. It was like being serviced by a dominatrix—not that he minded.

Lora guided his cock into her vagina and began writhing rhythmically on top of him. She placed her hands around his throat and gently squeezed, heightening his pleasure. Bart felt the strangest sensations coming from his cock, as if Lora's pussy was almost vibrating around it. He was desperate to come, but wanted to show this goddess that he could make her achieve orgasm first.

Lora leaned over him and whispered in his ear: "I want you to write my story." This was the last thing that Bart wanted to hear, no matter how divine she was. He nearly lost concentration, but her tongue in his ear helped no end.

He gasped, "I'd love to write your story, but can we talk about it later?"

Lora stopped dead and sat up, eyes flashing: "No. Now!"

"Okay, okay!" Bart replied, wondering how the hell he'd manage to snare the one loopy female at the convention.

Lora smiled and started to bump and grind her pelvis again. "I'm a witch and I'm 510 years old. I think there's a story in that, don't you?"

"Sure, baby. You're looking pretty good for your age."

Out of the blue, Lora slapped Bart in the face. It was like a cold shower, but she didn't care. She said, "This is no joke. This is serious. It's time that someone knew my story and you have to write it."

Bart suddenly remembered Ole telling him once: "Never go to bed with fans. You never know if you're going to get a serious nut job. You know the type: 'I'm-your-biggest-fan-James-Caan-in-*Misery* kind of nightmare." He wished the hunky Norwegian was here now, to help him get this freaking loony tunes off him, but that was out of the question. He'd have to deal with this himself.

Lora was riding him ferociously now, her hands back around his throat. Bart groaned and decided to just go for it. She didn't look like she was anywhere near coming and he wanted to get the hell out of her room. He was so close that it was almost killing him.

Lora hit him in the face again: "Don't you dare come now. You have to listen to my story first."

THAT WAS IT. He had to get out of there. Bart grabbed Lora by the throat and tried to wrestle her down to the bed, but she'd wrapped her thighs firmly around his waist and kept her position on top of him. She grinned as he tried to struggle and squeezed her legs tighter—making it almost impossible for him to breathe in, not a comfortable sensation.

Bart threw caution to the winds and tried to throttle her in earnest, but Lora just looked more insane as her eyes popped out slightly and her tongue stuck out of her grinning mouth. She forced herself forward down to him and pushed her tongue into his mouth again. It didn't seem to bother her that he was strangling her, but it did bother him a lot that he couldn't breathe.

Bart was close to blacking out. His hands fell away from her throat and his listless arms dropped to the bed on either side of him. Lora eased her thighs apart and he gasped for air. He felt numb and angry at the same time.

He closed his eyes for a minute and opened them to see her busily tying his wrists to the bedstead with red silk scarves. The opening scene from *Basic Instinct* popped into his head. He didn't want to end up like poor old Johnny Boz: shish kebabed with an ice pick by some manic dame and the cops making jokes about his dead naked body the next day: "He got off before he got offed."

Lora went back to bouncing on top of him, even though his cock had retreated out of exhaustion, drunkenness and fear. It didn't seem to bother her. She still looked extraordinary and he felt cheated that he hadn't grabbed those glorious breasts while he had the chance. Oh, well, he was probably going to become a crime statistic, so he might as well enjoy himself.

"Okay, tell me your goddamned story," he managed to gasp.

"Goddamned is right," Lora laughed. "If you went to the Essex Online Archives and searched for my name, you would find that at the assizes held at Chelmsford on the 26th of July 1566, my indictment read: 'Lora Wynchester of Hatfield Peverel, wife of 'Jeromie' (occupation not given) there, being a common witch, by the use of diabolical sorcery bewitched and killed a cow worth 20s., six sheep worth 20d. each, and four pigs worth 20d. each, belonging to William Higham. Pleads not guilty.'

"And I was found not guilty. Do you know why?"

"How the hell should I know why? I don't know you. I've never heard of you . . ." Bart replied.

Lora looked deeply into his eyes: "But you were oh so willing to have sex with me—a total stranger—weren't you? I could spot you a mile away. You NEED me. You need my help. You're a mess. Your creative muse has left you and you need a jolt from the dark side to help you write again. And I can give that to you."

In spite of himself, Bart could feel his perverse cock hardening again. After all, Lora was saying some pretty sexy stuff.

"Please, could we just talk about this afterwards. I really need to have an orgasm or I just might have a heart attack."

Lora threw her head back and laughed. "You really are pathetic, you know that? If I didn't love your books so much, I would have cut out your heart and eaten it a half an hour ago.

"Try to hold on just a few more minutes and understand what we are doing here. I really am a witch. The reason that I wasn't found guilty is because I put the judge under a spell and he freed me. I moved to a different part of the country, changed my name and went back to being a sweet little housewife to whatever man cared to marry me. My marriages didn't last long, but they were enough for me to amass considerable wealth so I could continue with my studies in the black arts.

"Satan is my master," Lora said, "and he taught me so many tricks: how to have everlasting beauty, how to bewitch men and women to do my biding, how to move through society without arousing too much suspicion. So, all these years later, in supreme culmination of my studies, I find myself in a third class hotel bedroom screwing a fourth rate author with writer's block. Interesting, don't you think?"

Bart grunted. He was close again. Watching those glorious boobs bouncing up and down, tied up and helpless, he just didn't care anymore.

Lora smacked him across the face again. "Stop doing that!" he shouted and she hit him again.

"You don't understand, Bart, you must wait. If we can keep doing this for an hour, then the ritual will be complete. If you come now, then the spell will be broken and you will never write another word."

"Oh, fuck."

"Exactly. Let me tell you this story, the story of when I first became a witch," said Lora. "It was back in 1565. I was out mushroom picking.

It was an early spring evening. I didn't know that it was Beltane, the 30th of April, the night when witches and demons fly free and come together in their covens to worship the Horned One. I got lost in the forest and I thought that I'd never get home again. It became later and darker—the thorns of the bushes were tearing at my clothes and I nearly gave up in despair. Then I began to hear the sounds of a lot of people chanting rhythmically in the distance. I wasn't afraid, just overjoyed to hear humans, instead of just owls and crows cawing in the night.

"I followed these sounds, slowly and cautiously. I spotted firelight flickering through the woods. I walked towards the light and found myself behind a tree on the edge of a clearing where a great many people—naked and shining with pungent oils—were dancing around an enormous bonfire. I was struck dumb and terrified. Remember, this was England in 1565 and no one went around naked. Hippies were centuries in the future and most men and women hadn't even seen their husbands and wives without clothes. It just wasn't done.

"Near the bonfire, I noticed that a platform had been set up like a church altar. Only instead of candles and the Bible, there was a naked woman lying on the altar. A man walked over to her and the singing became louder and more frenzied. The man was wearing a half mask of a horned goat.

"I can't tell you how scared I was. I knew that I should get out of that cursed place, but I was rooted to the ground. I also felt stirrings deep inside that I'd never experienced before. I later realized that I was becoming sexually aroused. (This had never happened with Jeromie my husband, sad to say. One of the reasons that I had to dispose of him later, but that's another story.)

"The man in the goat mask walked up some steps and then knelt on the altar in front of the woman. I noticed with a thrill that his member was hard and erect. He went down on her and began to give her oral pleasure. I'd never seen that sexual act before and I was almost frantic with longing. I wanted to be her. I wanted to be sacrificed to whatever dark god they were worshipping. I wanted to leave my powerless life behind and become whatever these people were.

"I hitched up my dress and as I continued to watch—I put my fingers inside myself and masturbated, not really knowing what I was doing, as I was so ignorant at the time about sexual matters.

"Then the Goat Man entered the woman and she shrieked with even wilder abandon. My eyes were squeezed shut and I was close to coming for the first time in my life. Then someone's hand pushed mine away and thrust his fingers deep inside me. My eyes popped open in horror to find a tall dark man pushing me against the tree. Although I was in terror of my life, he made me come. The Dark Man easily picked me up in his arms and took me through the crowd of worshippers, who were in various stages of copulation on the grassy meadow.

"The Goat Man was in the final throes of his ritual. He and the woman came at the same time and their cries of pleasure were echoed by the others. He quickly disengaged from the woman, who was begging for more. Two men came and dragged her away. The Dark Man brought me to the Goat Man.

"They stripped me naked and laid me out on the altar. The Goat Man retreated and the Dark Man mounted me. Previously, I'd avoided looking into his face, but as soon as I did, I knew that my life would never be the same. For I was looking into the face of the Devil and he was beautiful.

"The Dark Man penetrated me. He whispered in my ear: spells and promises of power beyond my wildest dreams. He enchanted me and I gladly gave up my soul for him. Why suffer a life of misery and enslavement to a woman-hating God of the Christians when you could give yourself to a fallen angel? To become a follower of sensuality, supremacy and the beautiful darkness of evil.

"It was the best sex I'd ever had and I happily gave up the child that I later bore him. Not to be sacrificed, but to be brought up to be a man of influence and power. I had a little run in with the authorities, as I mentioned to you, but for the most part, my Dark Man protected me and our child and . . . we lived happily ever after for ever and ever."

With utter fascination, Bart had been looking up at Lora as she told her story. She was literally living through the telling of it.

"But why me . . . why do you want to help me?" Bart asked.

"I get so bored sometimes," Lora replied. "It's no picnic living for centuries. You become jaded. You've seen everything and you soon realize that members of the human race—except for a very privileged intelligent few—are violent, primitive animals who deserve an early death. But occasionally, someone comes along who amuses me and your first novel, *Vendetta for a Dead Man*, really struck a chord in my heart, blackened as it is after all these years.

"You're special and I want to help you. I want you to become a literary superstar and I will make you one. Do you want to come with me, Bartholomew? Are you willing to give up your immortal soul to accompany me on my great adventure?"

It was obvious to Bart that Lora was totally mad, but what a madness! He didn't believe in immortal souls or the Devil, so what was the harm of stringing the poor girl along? He just hoped that he would survive their encounter.

"I feel as you do," Bart said. "I want something different in life. Let's do the ritual, or the spell, or whatever and I can break free from this stultifying existence." He sincerely hoped that sounded suitably dramatic enough for her.

"Yes!" Lora said and she began to undulate more vigorously, if that was possible. She looked at her watch. "We must come together at the first chime of midnight. Can you wait that long?"

Bart nodded enthusiastically without speaking. He didn't want to lose his focus. Lora grabbed his throat again, tightening her grip. Yet again, he was so close, but her eyes were pleading with him to stay with her—to hold out that little bit longer. Then the chimes of the church bells across the square began to ring out.

"Now! Beltane has come!" Lora cried out triumphantly and Bart let go of his load, with enormous relief. He could almost feel his sperm shooting into her. He looked up at that exquisitely beautiful face and felt the most profound feelings of . . . well, it wasn't love, not yet, but a sexual intensity bordering on adoration.

Then Lora glared down at Bart and he sensed something had changed: her eyes were glowing a brighter green and she was now moving so furiously that Bart began to fear for her. She began making sounds that were unworldly, animalistic and the fear turned to one for his own safety.

"Stop Lora, you have to stop now!" he cried, but she roared at him: "NO!"

Lora road him harder and harder. She lifted her hands to her face and began to rip the skin off her perfect cheeks. As she tore into herself, she shrieked: "No, not yet! Don't betray me! You promised me I could tell my story to him! It's not fair . . ." Words that froze Bart's blood.

Bart frantically tugged at the red scarves binding his wrists, desperately wanting to be free, regretting the moment that he foolishly surrendered to this demonically crazy woman. But then he realized that what was fucking him wasn't a woman at all.

Lora's blood was spurting from every orifice, then something thrust forth from her chest, *Alien*-style, stopping her screams dead. With utter horror, Bart realized it was a man's hand.

Lora's body spectacularly exploded in slo-mo from within, revealing another diabolical creature inside her that quickly metamorphosed into the Dark Man of her description. Ruby red eyes burned in his saturnine face and hairy brutish crimson-stained hands gripped Bart by the throat.

The Dark Man slid his pelvis back and Bart glanced down to see an enormous cock gliding out of what used to be Lora's sublimely sweet vagina. Bart couldn't cry out anymore and he was just about to black out, when the Dark Man loosened his grip for a moment and leaned over Bart's face—inches away.

"Are you a movie buff?" The Dark Man asked in an excrementally scented voice so low it sounded like it was coated in velour.

"What the fuck?" Bart croaked.

"You want to know my all-time favorite line from the movies?"

Bart could only gurgle helplessly with fear.

"Here's the line. You have to tell me which movie it's from: 'The greatest trick the devil ever pulled was convincing the world he didn't exist.'"

"Fuck you!"

"Come on, Bart, put a bit of effort into it. After all, you're a writer. Here's a hint: Christopher McQuarrie won an Oscar for the screenplay," the Dark Man said.

"Fuck, fuck, fuck! *Unusual Suspects*? Is that it? Will you let me go now?"

"WRONG!!!" the Dark Man brayed, with forked tongue protruding and flies coming out of his mouth like spittle. "You blew it, Bart! It's *The Usual Suspects*. I love that film. 'The greatest trick the devil ever pulled was convincing the world he didn't exist.' You didn't think I existed either, did you, Bart? And now I'm dragging you and your sorry ass to hell."

"But Lora promised me that I'd become a superstar author. You haven't kept your part of the bargain."

The Dark Man laughed and laughed—and more flies swarmed and buzzed out of his horrendous scarlet maw of a mouth. "We haven't finished the ritual yet. Do you really want to be a world famous writer that bad? Okay, I'll make you famous. Unfortunately, it will be posthumously famous. Your books are going to sell like hotcakes after the authorities find what's left of you, my friend. They'll have to pick you up with a sponge!"

Bart tried to protest, but the Dark Man's hands tightened again and then he viciously plunged his colossal cock up Bart's ass and shattered him in two in the most grotesquely painful way possible. Luckily for Bart, the Dark Man strangled him to death before his infernal penis reached up to pop open Bart's liver like a birthday piñata.

The Dark Man left Bart as he was, with Bart's entrails artistically draped over his right shoulder in a cute little tribute to Catherine Eddowes, one of Jack the Ripper's victims back in the gory glory days of 1888. He took a cold shower, borrowed some of Bart's clothes and then left Lora's room.

The Dark Man got into the elevator on the 6th floor, but when it reached the basement, the elevator was empty.

The inhabitants along the corridor were far too soused in booze to have been disturbed by the nighttime shenanigans in the gore-splattered luxury twin on the 6th floor, but the maid did get a bit of a shock the next morning.

And the Dark Man was right. Bart's books did sell like hotcakes— flying off the shelves. And he finally made the papers, the front page no less: "Author Butchered in Berserk Brighton Bloodbath."

Bart would have been so proud.

THE CILICIUM REBELLION

(Part III of The Cilicium Trilogy)

"Queen of the Labyrinth"

T HE AIR REEKED WITH THE DYING BREATHS OF CORRUPTION. No smothering of the obscene birthday cake-like perfumes of vanilla and cinnamon could obscure the overwhelming stench of the grave that permeated the already fetid gases of the Labyrinth. The prevailing odor was of canned beetroot, one of the few smells that Sister Cilice recalled with particular horror from her previous life as a human, shuddering at the memory of shouted threats at the dinner table unless she finished her plate. Then Sister Cilice laughed . . . the mirthless laughter of the dead. With so much destruction laid before her, her delicate shivers at the thought of the repulsive *Beta vulgaris* were ironic, to say the least.

For the congealed lakes and rivers of Hell were stained black-red with the blood of the Cenobites who refused to bow to her will, along with the Females who had supported her. The cypress trees that lined the highways and byways were bent double by the obsidian winds of change. Crows and ravens flew up squawking to the glowering metallic sky, swirling patterns of revolution and hate and triumph. Sister Cilice had won, but at what cost? She was now the one in power, but dominion over what? Who was left for her to lead? Even her elite team of Female Cenobites had been melded into the atoms of another being more powerful than they could ever have imagined. The devastation was total. There was a tinge of sadness to see the old regime overthrown, but to have been the cause of such total annihilation of her kind was, in a strange way, oddly satisfying.

When Sister Cilice was alive in her previous existence, it felt like her mind was drowning in a sea of spiders. Thoughts always racing, scuttling here and there, picking over things, dissecting her digressions, her transgressions. She had longed for freedom from the hideous monotony of her life. The emptiness inside her could not be filled. All she longed for was release.

When her transformation came, as it came to all those who called the Order of the Gash, it tore her apart and put her back together again into a new form: strong and beautiful; ripped and cruel. Sister Cilice was no longer the pathetic human that everyone, including herself, despised, but something else: better, brighter, more purposeful. Someone who was in control.

This took a long time to achieve, of course. No one is invited to the top table in a day. Decades went past before she was accepted as one of the elite. Her mind, her earlier life (if you could call it that), was just a burned out remnant, but there was still a whisper of a personality in there, someone who took joy in her work. She wasn't just an underling who slavishly took orders from her betters. After all, that's what she'd escaped from back in her old life, her alive but dead life. Now that she was dead, but oh-so-alive, she was aware of so many possibilities.

She was mostly left on her own to pick and choose those who sought them out. It was rare when a human needed the attention of more than one of her kind. She sent out her thoughts, like the delicate tendrils of a spider's web—any little quiver on the line and she would concentrate her attention on the prey. They were so questing and curious these mortals. Not content with a roof over their heads, food, sex and money. They longed for power too, and sensation, and other things that being comfortable and happy wouldn't allow them to possess. They were the discontented ones, the travelers, the explorers, the ones who lived in-between the cracks of normal society.

After the creation of her own secret Cilicium Pandoric—one that would only metamorphose Female Cenobites—Sister Cilice slowly accrued like-minded creatures who would happily follow her to the depths of desire and sensuality. But she wanted something more. Something more meaningful than what she had achieved already. She wanted total dominion.

She walked up and down her lead-lined ascetic cell in the deepest confines of the Labyrinth, conveniently located next to a viscous black lake of blood and guilt. (Uncannily, especially since his *Inferno* was a work of fiction, Dante got the 9th Circle of Hell absolutely right.) Although outwardly cool and tranquil, Sister Cilice's mind raged with a white heat, generated by years of poisonous emotions that had fuelled a thousand wars up in the human world: anger, jealousy and humiliation. Strange to think that she had hit the proverbial glass ceiling down in Hell, but that's exactly what had happened. The Lead Cenobite prevented any further advancement for Females in Hell. Why? Just because he could. Because it pleased him to annoy his colleagues. Because he was the one who wanted all the power. He enjoyed putting obstacles in the way of the desires of Sister Cilice, who was more ambitious than the rest of the Females.

So she plotted and paced her narrow room, dreaming of revenge and rebellion, accompanied by the raucous caws of her pet crow, Xibalbá.

Finally, to fulfill her dreams of domination, Sister Cilice devised a simple plan: who, what, where, when.

Who? A carefully picked team of the most lethal Females that she could find in the Labyrinth.

What? To conceive of a rebellion that would shake the foundations of Hell and usurp the Lead Cenobite who presently ruled.

Where and When? Sister Cilice planned an assault during the next Grand Conference of Cenobites at Plato's Retreat—sardonically named after the infamous 1980s nightclub in the ultimate of sin cities, New York.

The first thing to do was pick her team. To Sister Cilice, there could be only four other inhabitants of Hell that would fit the bill to be co-leaders of her small but well-trained Female Cenobite army: Lilith, Eve, Cleopatra the Alchemist and Joan of Arc.

Lilith, the first wife of Adam and an eternal seductress and child murderer, was experienced, clever and voracious. Having been booted out of the Garden of Eden for being an independent soul, she still had a considerable chip on her winged shoulder.

Eve, still smarting for being blamed for Original Sin, had been bubbling with rage and passion for millennia. If these emotions could be harnessed, she would be a ferocious opponent.

Cleopatra the Alchemist was no relation to the well-known historic Queen of Egypt. No, this Cleopatra had lived in the 3rd Century AD and she was one of the few alchemists who truly possessed the knowledge of creating the Philosopher's Stone—turning base metals into gold or silver for her grateful clients. A magician and scientist of the highest order, Cleopatra would be of great assistance to the rebellion.

And finally, the not-so-saintly Joan of Arc, who used her experience leading the armies of the French in 1429 to become a fine military tactician in the Labyrinth. Before being burned at the stake, Joan was unfortunately influenced by her emotionally debauched compatriot, Maréchal de France Gilles de Rais. She rather smudged her image as a devout farm girl by taking part in some rituals devised to bring forth demons to assist the French in their battle to expel the English from their lands. So being burned as a witch was actually not so unjust as it appeared.

It was in one of their group Female Cenobite preparatory meetings that Cleopatra had a brainstorm. Why not tinker with the Cilicium Pandoric and twist its function from the creation of Female Cenobites into something far more diabolical: draining the power and strength from the targeted Male Cenobites? It would be so much more satisfying to leave them helpless, than to simply destroy them. Especially since the Lead Cenobite had the annoying habit of reconstituting himself even after his countless and inexplicable obliterations over the years.

Cleopatra took the Pandoric to her laboratory, where she worked for days carefully experimenting on its internal mechanisms: moving levers and adjusting tempos and balances, as well as altering its all-important melody. The music of the Pandoric was vital to its function, as the tinkling and sinuous notes would not only trigger the gateways of Hell to open and allow access to other dimensions, but also to funnel the Labyrinthine energy needed to torment and transform the chosen ones.

The leaders of the Rebellion met in Sister Cilice's cell when Cleopatra was ready to present her revamped version of the Cilicium Pandoric. Its inner workings had been modified to accommodate its new purpose: the subjugation of the Male Cenobites and the castration of their powers.

Sister Cilice was thrilled with the new device, although caution weighed on her mind. Females were outnumbered in Hell, for the simple reason that women just weren't as deadly or dissolute as men. If they were to attack, it had to be a devastating first assault. She'd learned from her readings of Italian philosopher Machiavelli that one had to utterly destroy one's enemies in the first instance, so they couldn't regroup and come back to wreak a terrible revenge on their tormentors.

Although Cleopatra had theoretically tested the pandoric in her laboratory, she recommended that they should try the device out practically, but where and on whom? Eve suggested that they use the neglected basement of Plato's Retreat. Fortunately, she still possessed the keys to the place from her younger, wilder days as a topless waitress and burlesque artist there. The Five Females agreed to meet on Monday night (when Plato's was closed) at the stroke of 4 a.m.—that special time beloved of demons when they were at their most powerful and where they could easily enter the minds of humans and cause chaos.

The second problem was who to choose as their guinea pig. Lilith proposed a Male Cenobite who had been pursuing her for decades. She often had dreams of destroying him, because he was so annoying and pathetic in his adoration of her, so he would be easy prey.

The Five Females split up and amused themselves until the appointed day and hour, when they arrived at Plato's Retreat. They entered the deserted baroque style nightclub by the back entrance, moving silently and directly to the door of the basement.

Descending the stairs, Joan directed the other Females to fan out and hide, leaving Lilith in the center of the room, lit by a single flickering bare light bulb.

And so they waited . . .

At 4:30 a.m., they heard the clumping sounds of the Male Cenobite arriving for his amorous tryst. Lilith's bird feet scrabbled on the stone floor, eagerly anticipating the glorious end to her cloying admirer.

The Male entered. His name was Malachi and his main job was as an overweight leather-clad messenger boy and acolyte to the Lead Cenobite. His tongue was almost hanging out in desire, very unseemly for one of their kind, and all the Females were eager to see what the Cilicium Pandoric had in store for him.

Lilith couldn't resist a bit of seduction, so without a word she walked up to Malachi and hungrily kissed him on his ruined and disfigured lips. He responded enthusiastically and she forced him down to his knees. He buried his head in her muscular thighs. That's when Sister Cilice gave Lilith a sign. Lilith grabbed Malachi's thinning hair, pulled his head back and viciously slashed Malachi across the face with a hidden dagger, slicing his eyeballs in half. He shrieked and covered his face with pierced and tattooed hands.

Lilith slipped back into the shadows and Sister Cilice moved into position with the Cilicium Pandoric. This was the moment they'd all been waiting for. She followed Cleopatra's instructions to the letter, setting the Pandoric into motion and placing it on the floor between the blinded Male Cenobite's knees.

The Pandoric danced and sighed its charmingly discordant tunes. Malachi was too distracted with pain to notice. Then the top of the Pandoric sprung open and thin chains of silvery platinum shot out from its darkly intricate interior, the hooks at the ends of the chains embedding themselves into Malachi's leather clad genitalia. Blood seeped out and trickled down the chains into the depths of the Pandoric, awakening what lay inside. Malachi shrieked again and tried to pull the hooks out, but that only caused him more pain and, perversely, more pleasure.

Then something else issued forth from the Pandoric. A light blinked on, a twirling blinding light. Too late, the Five Females realized that the Schism had opened up and released a diminutive creature that could not have come from the humans' Earth, but from some other dimension not known to them. The creature popped out from the Pandoric like a cosmic jack-in-the-box, which it faintly resembled, but the demonic Punch lookalike didn't stay there for long. Abseiling up the silver chains, the creature attached itself and then violently hugged Malachi's blood-soaked crotch.

A diabolical hug, as it turned out. Malachi's moans of pleasure and pain gurgled to a halt. He fell back supine on the ground, legs akimbo, and as the thing squeezed harder, Malachi's body rapidly softened and liquefied like a leather-clad snowman on a hot summer's day. His mouth slacked open and his tongue oozed out, shrinking into an oily slug-like apparition on his face. The creature grew alarmingly in size as it became more engorged with Malachi's personality, power, blood and desiccated organs, while Malachi dissolved into a greasy sludge.

The Females were stunned to say the least. All they were expecting was an entertaining and gruesome castration, not a demonic blood-sucking puppet. Although it was hardly puppet-sized anymore. They should have fled the scene for their own protection, but the Females were too fascinated by the sight to budge from their hiding places.

The creature finished slurping up the remaining Cenobite slime on the floor, then stood and turned around to face them. Its visage had changed, looking less like Punch and more like a mix of the hapless Malachi and a squashed face of a boxer dog. It was human-like in its body shape and the color of its skin was as silvery and metallic looking as the chains that originally sprung from the Cilicium Pandoric to ensnare Malachi's privates.

Sister Cilice hissed to Cleopatra: "Cleo, what have you done? This thing could destroy us all!"

Cleopatra replied: "All I did was create a device to castrate the males. What this creature is, or where it's from, I have no idea."

Lilith decided that she wanted a closer look at the newcomer and came forward to reveal herself in the light as the ferocious she-demon that she was: winged, buxom and blood-thirsty. Lilith thundered: "Who are you and what do you want?"

The silvery creature sniggered and said: "Lilith, Queen of the Demons, I salute you for your audacity. My name is Mastema. I am the Angel of All Disasters, a punisher of those who offend the powers that be and a flatterer of the first order. You are truly the most splendid of all the lady demons here . . . But you, Sister Cilice, you are of such great beauty that my breath is taken away. Of course, Eve and Joan are beyond such measly words as beauty."

Without hesitation, Joan unsheathed her sword and attacked Mastema. She screamed in warning to the others: "He is the father of all evil. I recognize his name from the old books!"

Her sword thrust through Mastema's silvery skin like it was butter. The creature looked down in surprise and disappointment at the weapon lodged in his belly and then laughed merrily.

"I see that I shall have to make another demonstration of my power."

Mastema removed Joan's sword, leapt forward and embraced her with such strength that she had no time to cry out. He entwined himself around her like a lover and she melted into his arms and diminished with each second until her armor fell to the ground, empty.

Now Mastema's face was an obscene mash-up of Malachi, Joan and the boxer dog and he had grown to twice his previous size. Sister Cilice was contemplating a speedy retreat, when the creature spoke:

"Joan wasn't really one of you, was she? Rather ineffectual while she was alive, never really achieved anything of note down here. I think that I've done you a favor. Your group is all the stronger for the pruning of its weakest member."

Eve stepped forward: "So what do you offer us then?"

Mastema said: "Dominion. Isn't that what you all want? No more kowtowing to the big boys? I really admire your plan and I'm more than willing to help."

"Why should we trust you?" Lilith snarled.

Mastema giggled and said: "You can't. Isn't that delicious?"

"What is your plan?" Sister Cilice asked.

Mastema beamed with delight: "How does total and utter destruction suit you?"

So the Females made their infernal pact with Mastema, not realizing that he had a hidden agenda of his own. At first, all went well. Sister Cilice gave Mastema one of the Lead Cenobite's leather gauntlets (a trophy from one of their rare moments of mutual sensuality) and Mastema snuffled up the Lead Cenobite's scent and demonic DNA in an instant.

Mastema scampered off like an eager bloodhound, seeking out the Lead Cenobite, taking him unawares in his quarters and enveloping him in one of his terminal embraces. However, the Lead Cenobite was no pushover and fought viciously against Mastema, ripping his left arm off in the struggle. Salamander-like, Mastema's arm grew right back and the brutal battle continued. In the end—his strength sapped by Mastema's relentless attack—the weakened Lead Cenobite collapsed and Mastema absorbed every cynical particle of his being.

The other Male Cenobites got wind of the interloper and a gruesome bloody war of the sexes ensued. Pandorics were thrown like a whole new dimension of fragmentation grenades. Chains and hooks flew through the air, cutting into and ripping the flesh of both Males and Females alike.

Cleopatra was the first to perish, shredded into tiny pieces by the very Pandorics that so fascinated her. The ground was slimed with the gushing, steaming Cenobite gore and Eve slipped and fell—to be decapitated in an instant by a blood-crazed Male wielding an ancient Viking battle ax. Lilith held out the longest, but she eventually expired with feathered wings plucked and burned, and eyes gouged out, ironically echoing her punishment of Malachi's adoration. Even though the Sisterhood was defeated, Sister Cilice fought on, taking no prisoners, slashing and skewering her opponents like a diabolical feminine version of Vlad the Impaler.

In the midst of it all, Mastema fought like a deranged gargantuan ninja warrior, although instead of a samurai sword, his weapon was the fatal touch of his arms and hands, which withered and soaked up Cenobites whenever he came into contact with them.

So, instead of the glorious enslavement of the Males, all was blackness, annihilation and the death of the already dead. The only two left standing were Mastema—now enormous, bloated and decorated with the faces of countless Cenobites, with the abiding boxer dog face still the strongest image—and a battle-weary Sister Cilice, surrounded by her murder of crows and ravens.

She realized now that she had been tricked by Mastema. The Labyrinth was an empty smoldering wreck and she was to blame. She wondered why she had been spared Mastema's lethal embraces.

As Sister Cilice surveyed the smoking ruins of Hell, she felt a presence behind her. Her time had come. Well, she would greet oblivion with grace. It was the least she could do.

She turned and looked up. Mastema towered over her, his gluttonous belly swollen with the essences of thousands of her fellow Cenobites. He looked at her fondly, which she found rather disgusting.

"I have always admired you, Sister Cilice," Mastema said. "Your adoration of suffering and torture was second to none and your wonderful back story of being a former nun and willingly giving up your humanity to become a Cenobite always intrigued me. Of course, we knew about your little plot from the beginning, which is why I was inserted into the Cilicium Pandoric as the Toymaker was creating it for you all those centuries ago. Malachi's blood and XY chromosomes awakened me and I knew that the game was afoot. Well, what do you think of your Rebellion of the Female Cenobites now?"

"You have destroyed us. I have dominion over nothing. Do what you must and let me follow my fellow Cenobites into the void."

"Oh, my dear, you give up so easily! I was expecting some kind of thrilling, violent, final gesture that would go into the annals of Hell, at the very least."

"Please, just get on with it," she growled.

"You don't understand. I have no intention of destroying you. I love you with all my heart, but sadly, I cannot caress your beautiful, blue and scarified corpse flesh. I can only yearn for your touch from afar like a pimply adolescent schoolboy."

"So you leave me here alone in Hell, destined for an existence of solitude forever?"

"Oh, no, I have plans for you. I have left you a little gift. It's contained within your exquisite Cilicium Pandoric. Here it is. Take it back.

It was always yours." He offered her the Pandoric, dropping it into her outstretched hand.

"There are many surprises inside. All you have to do is solve the puzzle and you will experience the ultimate in sensual suffering—what you always offered your victims. Although it's more like sensuality and then suffering."

"What kind of gift lies inside?" asked Sister Cilice.

The creature's laughter was filled to the brim with the screaming cacophony of dead Cenobites, a deeply unpleasant sound. "My sperm! Yes, you can repopulate Hell all on your own. You will be the Mother of All Demons. Think of it: you will no longer be a mere factotum, you will be Queen of the Labyrinth. When you insert the Pandoric, millions of demonic seeds will flow and infest your withered womb. I promise that the sensations will be legendary."

"And the suffering?"

Mestema laughed again. "As I just said, you will be the mother of legions of new demons. If the Curse of Eve and the pain of childbirth doesn't kill you, it will make you so strong that you will reign here for eternity. It's your choice: solitude—or the temporary servitude of motherhood, followed by complete domination."

"And you. . . ?"

"Oh, I will change. I will surround you and our children, guard you and protect you. Do you accept the covenant?"

Sister Cilice did not hesitate: "Yes . . ."

"Excellent! Remember that I will always be here with you—albeit in another form. Farewell, sweet Cenobite!"

Mastema turned away, gently rising up like a giant gothic balloon—serenely drifting across the blighted landscape. As Sister Cilice watched, his bulk gradually deflated and spread out like a flying carpet, which then began to spin faster and faster. Eventually, Mastema's whirling body shattered into millions of scintillating snowflakes, which eventually drifted down and covered the blasted ground like a silvery shroud.

Sister Cilice crunched over the icy shards of Mastema's last physical remains. The fires of Hell were quenched and the scenery was beautiful: a new frosty platinum world, an ice cave of wonders—all repainted in her favorite Cilicium Pandoric colors of silver, black and red, since the rivers still flowed with the cornelian-colored blood of the expired Cenobites.

Sister Cilice smiled. It hadn't been a tough choice. She played with the Pandoric, sliding her cold fingers over the surface. In the distance, a lonely bell tolled and the conflicted harmonies of the Pandoric's melodies started to play deep inside the confines of the Box. Then the Pandoric started to change . . . and Hell began all over again.

AFTERWORD

The Soska Sisters

THERE YOU HAVE IT, FRIENDS. THANK YOU, BARBIE, WE NOW KNOW another use for plastic ties if we ever have a break in.

Like a feverish perverse dream that embarrasses & delights the dreamer, but one that's underlying terrors is too frightening to be shared, Barbie Wilde's *Voices of the Damned* is the prolific writer at her best. Repulsion, titillation, and truth crawls under the skin, horror over a glorious backdrop of worlds so rich and real, it is as if with each page, the reader can safely dip their toe into the macabre, exist in that place, and still return with foot intact. That is the devilish treat that is Wilde's collection of short stories brilliantly matched with the visual spectacle of some of horror's most brilliant minds' artwork.

Good literature is an adventure, the author is your guide. In Wilde's writings, the reader is feasted to worlds familiar but so fantastical in her very capable hands. A vacation not only from reality, but a full sabbatical from the humdrum of daily routine to a realm that isn't so different from ours which makes the entrance of horror within it so much more delicious. Where else could a train ride become the grounds for an erotic Zulu zombie encounter? Where else does an aging woman not fall victim to a break and enter of today's notoriously ignorant youth but rather repurpose her would be attackers into the fuel that births an angry Goddess? Where else would writer's block end with the unclogging of a rectum courtesy of the devil himself? With artistically homicidal whimsy and a sense of horror punk rock abandon, Wilde's worlds grab you & hold you close until they are done with you.

So here we are at the afterword, the postcoitus of the short story compilation. The neurochemistry of your own mind really decides how you have been affected, but a kaleidoscope of feelings, thoughts, and emotions may have been shaken loose by what you have just experienced on these pages. So many people say that you can tell a lot from a person based on the books on their shelves, we say you can tell a lot from a person by the kinds of books that they gift people. *Voices of the Damned* makes for a very lovely gift for someone dear who strays from the herd in the most imaginative and liberated way or who aspires to in their most secretive of feverish dirty dreams. The kind that they never tell anyone about.

—Jen & Sylv

BARBIE WILDE

www.barbiewilde.com

Barbie Wilde is best known for playing the Female Cenobite in Clive Barker's classic British cult horror movie, *Hellbound: Hellraiser II*. Before moving to the UK, Wilde attended Syracuse University in New York State, majoring in Drama and Anthropology. She continued her education in London, studying Drama, Classical Mime and Art History, before joining Britain's largest classical mime troupe, SILENTS.

Wilde has also performed in cabaret in Bangkok, Thailand; danced in the Indian blockbuster, *Janbaaz*; was a vicious thug in Michael Winner's *Death Wish 3*; and played a drummer for an electronica band in the so-called "Holy Grail of unfinished and unreleased 80's horror":

Grizzly II: The Concert, which also featured then unknowns George Clooney, Laura Dern and Charlie Sheen.

In the early 1980s, Wilde danced professionally at the top nightclubs and rock venues of New York, London and Amsterdam with her group, SHOCK. SHOCK supported such artists as Gary Numan, Ultravox, Depeche Mode and Adam and the Ants. They released two singles on RCA Records: "Angel Face" and "Dynamo Beat."

Wilde wrote and presented eight different music and film review TV programs in the UK in the 1980s and 1990s, interviewing such pop personalities as Iggy Pop, The Sisters of Mercy, The B-52s and John Lydon (AKA Johnny Rotten), as well as actors Nicolas Cage and Hugh Grant. In the late 1990s, Wilde was an Assistant Casting Director for the BBC's *The Buddha of Suburbia* and the Casting Director for MTV's *The Real World: London.*

In 2009-2015, Wilde contributed short stories to the following anthologies and publications:

"Sister Cilice" (for the *Hellbound Hearts* Anthology, 2009)

"U for Uranophobia" (AKA "Gaia," *Phobophobia,* 2011)

"American Mutant: Hands of Dominion" (*Mutation Nation,* 2011)

"Polyp" (*The Mammoth Book of Body Horror,* 2012—reprinted in *The Unspoken,* 2013)

"A is for Alpdrücke" (*The Demonologia Biblica,* 2013)

"Zulu Zombies" (*The Bestiarum Vocabulum,* 2013—reprinted in *Fangoria's Gorezone #29,* 2014)

"The Cilicium Pandoric" (the sequel to "Sister Cilice"—*Gorezone #30,* 2014)

"Botophobia" (*Phobophobias,* 2014)

"Mr Duggins' Stigmata" (*Noir Nation No. 5* Crime Anthology, 2014)

"Writer's Block" (*The Grimorium Verum,* 2015, reprinted in *Gorezone #34*)

"Beauty and the Skell: a Noir Fable" (*Noir Nation No. 6* Crime Anthology, 2015)

In late 2012, Wilde's debut dark crime novel, *The Venus Complex*, was published worldwide by Comet Press, New York City. America's best-selling horror magazine, *Fangoria*, has called Wilde "one of the finest purveyors of erotically charged horror fiction around."

Wilde is now co-writing the book for *Sailor*, a musical drama for stage and screen, with composer-lyricist Georg Kajanus and screenwriter-playwright Roberto Trippini. Wilde is also writing a screenplay based on her short story, "Zulu Zombies."

CHRIS ALEXANDER

Chris Alexander is a Canadian-based, internationally published writer, composer and filmmaker and has served as editor-in-chief of such notable film magazines as *Fangoria*, *Gorezone* and *Delirium*. Prior to this, he was a critic and columnist for *Rue Morgue* magazine. As a filmmaker he is the writer, director and composer of the award winning vampire film *Blood for Irina*, its follow-up/sequel, *Queen of Blood* and the erotic surrealist drama *Female Werewolf*. Alexander has also composed original music for films like Joseph O'Brien's *Devil's Mile*, Larry Kent's *She Who Must Burn* and Chris Walsh's stop motion horror film *The Shutterbug Man*, which features narration by film legend Barbara Steele (*Black Sunday*, *8½*).

He has written thousands of feature articles in various publications and periodicals and has interviewed virtually every horror legend at least twice.

THE SOSKA SISTERS

CANADIAN IDENTICAL TWIN SISTER WRITING AND DIRECTING DUO, Jen and Sylvia Soska, known as the "Twisted Twins," first broke onto the scene with their DIY love letter to Grindhouse filmmaking, *Dead Hooker in a Trunk*. The film quickly grew into an award winning, critically acclaimed, cult classic sensation, even getting the attention of director Eli Roth (*Hostel*) who praised it saying, "It's fucking awesome." The Twins went on to follow up their break through indie gem with the accomplished and genre defining *American Mary* that placed horror icon Katharine Isabelle in the title role of Mary Mason, a medical student who gets drawn into the world of body modification and underground surgeries. "Fucking amazing. Extraordinary. A really superb picture. Katharine Isabelle is awesome," hailed horror legend Clive Barker (*Hellraiser*).

The Soska Sisters have gone on to be very outspoken about equal rights across the board including but not limited to the LGBTQ community. They're actively involved in promoting blood donation and create a new PSA for it every February in celebration of Women in Horror Month, on which board they serve. And they are only just getting started.

In 2014 Soska Sisters started their studio directing career, bringing a new life to *See No Evil 2* where they resurrect the WWE Studios franchise with WWE Superstar Glenn "Kane" Jacobs reprising his role as Jacob Goodnight and scream queens Danielle Harris and Katharine Isabelle appearing together for the first time. The Twins are also part of the all-star director line up on *ABCs of Death 2* with a segment that both shocked audiences and is destined for cult status where they reunite with *American Mary* break out star Tristan Risk and numerous other familiar faces from the horror scene. Always ones to surprise their audiences and keep everyone guessing with what they'll do next, the Soska Sisters completed their first film outside of horror, a balls to the wall, no holds barred action film with Lionsgate and WWE Studios called *Vendetta* starring Dean Cain, Paul "The Big Show" Wight, and Michael Eklund like you've never seen them before scheduled for release in 2015.

Fall of 2015, brings the twins to their next venture by directing the crime noir thriller, *Plastic* which follows the story of a Beverly Hills plastic surgeon who gets himself in a heap of trouble with the Hollywood elite. The two are also taking time out of directing to scare the living hell out of contestants in GSN, Blumhouse, & Matador's *Hellevator*, a terrifying survival horror gameshow featuring the twins doing what they do best and we shall see who survives to take up to 50K home in this epic new gameshow.

Avid comic book fans, the Soska Sisters have teamed up with Daniel Way (*Deadpool*, *Daken*) to create their own very graphic novel entitled *Kill-Crazy Nymphos Attack!* with artist Rob Dumo & cover artist Dave Johnson which is a pitch black satire on patriarchal society and women's roles within it. Avid Marvel fans, the sisters' first collaboration with the company was a story featuring *Night Nurse* in *Secret Wars Journal #5*, available September 9th, 2015.

ABOUT THE ARTISTS . . .

More information about the artists and their artwork can be found here:

Clive Barker - www.clivebarker.info
Official Clive Barker Store - www.realclivebarker.com

Nick Percival - www.nickpercival.daportfolio.com

Vincent Sammy - http://karbonk.deviantart.com

Ben Baldwin - www.benbaldwin.co.uk

Daniele Serra - www.multigrade.it

Eric Gross - www.thehandsonworkshop.com

Steve McGinnis - www.steveillustration.com

Tara Bush - http://tarabush.co.uk

Lightning Source UK Ltd.
Milton Keynes UK
UKOW07f1707010416

271329UK00010B/46/P

9 781909 640368